PSYCE

PSYCHO
LOVE
COMEDY

3

MURDER MAIDEN
AND THE FATAL FINAL

"I'M SORRY, AYAKA...
I'M TRULY SORRY FOR
MAKING YOU FEEL
THAT WAY."

All Hope Is Gone?
CORE CRISIS   QUESTION ONE

"OH, YOUR CALCULATIONS ARE WRONG AGAIN! YOU'RE NOT CAREFUL ENOUGH IN THE FINAL STEP, BIG BROTHER."

The Silence Is Suicide?

A DEADLY FLOWER IN EACH HAND

QUESTION TWO

"IT'S BEST
NOT TO RUSH.
SLOW DOWN
AND FOCUS
ON SOLVING IT.
CARELESS
MISTAKES ARE
YOUR GREATEST
ENEMY."

Ayaka Kamiya

THE MURDERERS OF PURGATORIUM REMEDIAL ACADEMY 3

PSYCOME

3
MURDER MAIDEN AND THE FATAL FINAL

Mizuki Mizushiro
x
Namanie

YEN
ON

NEW YORK

PSYCOME, Vol. 3: Murder Maiden and the Fatal Final
MIZUKI MIZUSHIRO

Translation by Nicole Wilder
Cover art by Namanie

This book is a work of fiction. Names, characters, places, and incidents are the product of the author's imagination or are used fictitiously. Any resemblance to actual events, locales, or persons, living or dead, is coincidental.

PSYCOME
©2013 MIZUKI MIZUSHIRO
All rights reserved.
First published in Japan in 2013 by KADOKAWA CORPORATION ENTERBRAIN.
English translation rights arranged with KADOKAWA CORPORATION
ENTERBRAIN through Tuttle-Mori Agency, Inc., Tokyo.

English translation © 2017 by Yen Press, LLC

Yen On
1290 Avenue of the Americas
New York, NY 10104

Visit us at yenpress.com
facebook.com/yenpress
twitter.com/yenpress
yenpress.tumblr.com
instagram.com/yenpress

First Yen On Edition: February 2017

Yen On is an imprint of Yen Press, LLC.
The Yen On name and logo are trademarks of Yen Press, LLC.

The publisher is not responsible for websites (or their content)
that are not owned by the publisher.

Library of Congress Cataloging-in-Publication Data
Names: Mizushiro, Mizuki, author. | Namanie, illustrator. |
Wilder, Nicole, translator.
Title: Psycome / Mizuki Mizushiro ; illustration by Namanie ;
translation by Nicole Wilder.
Other titles: Saikome. English
Description: First Yen On edition. | New York, NY : Yen On, 2016—
Identifiers: LCCN 2016005815 | ISBN 9780316272339 (v. 1 : paperback) |
ISBN 9780316398251 (v. 2 : paperback) | ISBN 9780316398268
(v. 3 : paperback)
Subjects: LCSH: False imprisonment—Fiction. | Science fiction. | BISAC: FICTION /
Science Fiction / Adventure.
Classification: LCC PZ7.1.M636 Ps 2016 | DDC 895.63/6—dc23
LC record available at http://lccn.loc.gov/2016005815

ISBNs: 978-0-316-39826-8 (paperback)
978-0-316-39827-5 (ebook)

1 3 5 7 9 10 8 6 4 2

LSC-C

Printed in the United States of America

PSYCOME

3

MURDER MAIDEN AND
THE FATAL FINAL

Contents

PSYCHO LOVE COMEDY

"Die!"

An iron pipe cut through the air, accompanied by a roar that was not at all suited to the lisping voice that made it. The tip of the pipe was en route to the bridge of a particular pierced nose, like always.

"Hya-haaaaaaaaaaaaa!"

In the next moment, however, that male student bent and twisted, avoiding the fierce blow. A violent wind blew across the bright red tips of his Mohawk as the pipe sailed past.

"......?!"

The classroom stirred at this unexpected development. Even Kurumiya, who had swung the pipe, opened both eyes wide.

Mohawk's eyes sparkled. With both hands, he currently gripped an enormous chainsaw. Readying the deadly weapon, holding it low as it reverberated with a heavy bass sound—*dudududududu*—Mohawk licked his lips.

"Gya-ha-ha-ha-ha! Victory is mine, widdle Kurumiyaaaaaa!" With a high-pitched war cry, he swung the chainsaw upward. The many whirring blades, spinning at incredible speed, carved a gash in the floor, threatening to split Kurumiya right in half from below. "Gya-ha!!"

Of course, this unthinkable thing did not come to pass. Easily shifting to avoid the blow, Kurumiya moved to grab hold of Mohawk's face with her empty hand.

"Gyaaaaaaah!" Despite his furious efforts, Mohawk could do nothing but struggle clumsily. Meanwhile the chainsaw blade, which had fallen to the side, continued to spin vigorously.

"Aaaaaahhh!"

Gagagagagaga. The chainsaw started to shave away at the desk of a nearby male student—Kyousuke Kamiya.

Kyousuke, who was nearly killed, fell out of his desk in a fright.

"Gaah!! Watch where you're touching, freak!"

"Huh?!"

The girl he had fallen on promptly slapped him.

Kurumiya, who held Mohawk in a clawhold, did not so much as

glance at that disturbance. "That you were able to avoid my iron pipe shows some growth, doesn't it, Mohawk? But remember this! An asshole like you will never take down someone like me, not in a hundred trillion yeeeaaars!!"

Furious, she struck the blackboard with her previously empty hand.

"Gya-haaaaaaaaaaaaaaahhh!!" The back of Mohawk's head ground into the surface of the board, cracks spidering out around it.

Releasing her grip on the problem child, his eyes now rolling back in his head, Kurumiya frowned. "Really...despite his thorough punishment during the prison camping trip, this little shit-pig seriously doesn't learn his lesson! And he stole my private property again. There's a limit to how far you can provoke me, you know... Breaking in even though I lock it up... Hey, medics! Clean up this garbage."

Responding to the teacher's orders, the white-clad group that had been on standby quickly collected Mohawk's body. They loaded him onto a stretcher and carried him off with a "heave-ho!" They also killed the engine of the chainsaw that had been just about to cut Kyousuke's desk apart, and carried it away as well.

"...Hey. How long do you plan to stay like that?"

The neighbor to Kyousuke's left—the girl with rust-red hair and eyes the same color and who had gotten involved when he fell on her—spoke up in an irritated voice.

She glared down at Kyousuke, who was clinging to her waist. "Hurry up and let go of me, you sex fiend!"

"Huh?!"

She hit him again.

"...Well, then. I'm resuming morning homeroom." Regaining her composure, Kurumiya began to distribute the printouts she had prepared.

Holding his cheek, which throbbed with pain, Kyousuke accepted a handout. On that piece of paper was written:

> Purgatorium Remedial Academy
> First Trimester Final Exam Schedule

Although there had been talk of exams, this was the first time one had actually been announced.

Looking around the noisy classroom, Kurumiya launched into a lengthy explanation. "Comprehensive evaluations at our institution happen three times each year in the form of final exams conducted at the conclusion of the first, second, and third trimesters. There are no midterm exams. Because of this, the scope of the exam is extensive, so each of you must work hard and review! The test is given over two days and covers ten subjects. Each exam takes sixty minutes, the same length as a class period."

A timetable was drawn on the printout, with instructions printed above and below. The first day would be Japanese language, social studies, English language, home economics, and art, while the second day would cover math, science, music, health education…and ethics. Except for the test on ethics and the broad scope of the exams, they seemed like surprisingly normal exams.

Nevertheless, it seemed that, even at this academy, students still found the prospect of exams to be depressing. The atmosphere in the classroom had grown noticeably gloomier. Amid the shadow that had fallen, Kurumiya continued to toll the bell:

"Now, a failing grade is anything below half of the average class score. As for what might happen in the unlikely event that you should get a failing grade in my class…well, you know the answer to that without me having to say it, don't you, my little piggies?"

Crushing the printout in her hand, she continued, her tone turning violent: "Don't think that your answer sheet will be the only thing stained red! The long vacation immediately following the exams will be canceled, and *various things* may end up broken during your supplementary lessons. And then, just try failing the supplementary examination! I'll teach you plenty besides the usual lessons! Fear and despair, shame and humiliation, torture techniques and execution methods from all over the world! I'll use your own bastard bodies as teaching materials!!"

—*Bam!* She slammed her fist down.

"…………"

The classroom returned to silence. Everyone in the room understood the situation clearly. These were no ordinary examinations. They were deadly tests on which they were being forced to gamble their lives.

Lording over her shuddering charges, Kurumiya added, "But…for the end-of-term exams, we don't just swing the rod. We also dangle the carrot! Anyone with superior grades will have their achievement recognized by being allowed to go out on *parole* in the free world during summer break! Of course, they'll be under probationary supervision, but for one whole week they'll have the chance to do whatever they please outside the institution! They can do anything they want to do, go anywhere they want to go, and see anyone they want to see…"

The atmosphere in the classroom responded to the juicy carrot being dangled before them. Shock, excitement, delight, agitation…

Among the students, the one who showed the most obvious reaction was—

"—Hey!"

Kicking his chair back, Kyousuke jumped to his feet, drawing the attention of his classmates. However, Kyousuke paid it no mind. He could only think about the announcement.

See anyone they want to see. Kurumiya had definitely said that.

"…Is that true?"

Eyes set on his grinning teacher, he demanded confirmation.

Kurumiya assented. "Of course! A teacher wouldn't tell lies to her students! While on parole, you will be free. As long as you adhere to the terms and conditions laid out by your probation officer, you will not be questioned as to what you do."

"…Terms and conditions?" Kyousuke inquired further. How many students would be rewarded with parole if their grades were high enough? He wanted to hear all the details up front.

Kurumiya toyed with a rolled-up printout. "On the basis of their total scores in all ten subjects, those who take *the top three spots in their grade* will qualify. As it says on your printout, that is the minimum requirement for parole. If, on top of that, the student does not exhibit any serious behavioral issues, then parole will be authorized. The criteria are not that strict, so you can relax. Though someone with delinquent behavior as bad as Mohawk's would likely be unequivocally rejected…"

Kurumiya's face distorted as she spat the words.

Mohawk, who had never even properly attended class, was the strongest contender for a failing mark. He would almost certainly be attending the supplementary lessons, and even thinking about it made Kurumiya miserable.

"Shit, that fuckin' pig-bastard! Die! Die, die, die!" she yelled, and as they watched her mutilate a printout, they found it impossible not to sympathize with her. "Hmph. Are those all your questions?"

"…Yes. Thank you." Nodding, Kyousuke sat back down. He read the information written on the printout. For someone like Kyousuke, who possessed only ordinary intelligence, ranking in the top three in his school year would not be an easy feat. The hurdle standing between him and parole was high.

It's not a matter of "can" or "can't." I will do it! Failing marks and supplementary lessons…I don't give a damn about all that! No matter what happens, I will be in the top three—!

He could be on the outside. Even if it was just one week, he would be able to go back and see her.

Her: his little sister, who was still awaiting his return. He wanted to apologize in person and set her mind at ease.

He would tell her that it might take time, but that he would definitely make it home.

He would ask her to be patient until then.

—I have to.

Purgatorium Remedial Academy was a strange school full of underage murderers. Kyousuke, who had been sentenced there on false charges, was now determined.

It was the last Friday in July. Ten days remained before the final exams. For the first time, Kyousuke would study like his life depended on it…

"Oh, and one more thing. I have a *serious announcement* to make."

"…Huh?"

Kyousuke, who had begun preparing for class, looked at Kurumiya to see what the matter was. Not "important" or "necessary," but *serious.*

He felt something strangely sinister in that.

Kurumiya cleared her throat. "Ahem.

"A new person will be joining our first-year Class A."

—A transfer student.

The classroom buzzed in response.

What could it mean to have a transfer student at this institution for murderers? And in July no less, just before exams? Kyousuke's premonition grew only darker.

"It's poor timing, but…in consideration of a special request from the transferee, and for certain personal reasons, measures were taken to authorize an extraordinary transfer." As she spoke, Kurumiya drew out a new iron pipe.

Thrusting the end, which was bent into a hook shape, toward the students, she continued:

"At the beginning of Golden Week this year, our transfer student entered their middle school classroom while a lesson was in session and fired a modified shotgun—or rather, had *planned* to. However, possibly because of a defect in how the gun was assembled, the shells did not discharge. The weapon misfired. Sadly, this person was arrested.

"In other words, it was attempted murder. Even so, their intent to kill was unmistakably real, and if the gun had not malfunctioned, there probably would have been enough victims to rival Kamiya's count of twelve… So, while zero people were actually killed, the brutality of this person's intentions could not be overlooked, and they were placed into our custody for rehabilitation."

Holding the iron pipe like a gun, Kurumiya mimicked shooting. "Bang!"

She had aimed it carefully at Kyousuke's forehead.

No blood gushed out, but plenty of sweat trickled down his face. *Bursting into a classroom holding a shotgun—that's too awful! And she's saying that someone like that is going to be in our class from now on? Ack! I won't be able to concentrate on the tests…!*

She had said that there were zero casualties, but that did not grant Kyousuke the slightest peace of mind. Judged by those actions, this new transfer student was not the kind of person he wanted anything to do with. But while Kyousuke trembled with fear, most of his classmates seemed to be growing excited.

"Wow, a shotgun is too cool! I want to try shooting one sometime, too. *Bang, bang, bang,* like that!"

"Hee-hee…a storm of bullets, then it rains blood…everything flooded bright red…hee-hee."

"A gun in Japan, they must be pretty disturbed…heh-heh! If it's a beautiful girl I'll give her a warm welcome, though."

"What a brutal person, seriously! Forget about roughing up old guys, that's a crime against humanity!"

And so on. Everyone talked to everyone else around them in one big racket.

However, the moment Kurumiya snapped one single word— "Quiet!"—the noise abruptly stopped.

The pupils were absolutely obedient to their teacher; that lesson had been beaten into their minds and bodies through repeated threats and violence.

"Well, there's no need for me to go on telling you this and that, eh? Why don't we get her to tell you the details directly from her own mouth? You bastards are probably curious, too, you sick bunch of murderers! You want to know what kind of person it is, the psycho chick who wouldn't hesitate to commit mass murder of her own school friends…heh-heh-heh."

Laughing, Kurumiya looked at the door in the front of the classroom. Everyone followed her gaze. "Okay, you're good," Kurumiya called out. "Get in here!"

Rattle, rattle, rattle… The sliding door opened.

"Here I come!"

Speaking in a high-pitched, out-of-tune voice, the transfer student finally appeared. The eyes of the other students, reflecting her figure, opened wide all at once.

…The transfer student was a young girl. She was short and incredibly slender; her delicate limbs, extending out of the sleeves and down from the skirt hem of her uniform, looked like they might snap at any moment. But what arrested everyone's eyes was not her body, but her *head*.

"Aww, I can barely see." Looking restlessly around the classroom, the transfer student entered. Where there should have been a human head, instead there was a light-brown, *freshly severed horse head*.

"_____"

Everyone stared at the unidentifiable horse person, dumbfounded.

The texture of the skin was incredibly realistic, including visible veins, and it shone wetly in the light. The half-open mouth, big nostrils, and bulging eyeballs struck quite an image.

"Eeeeeek!! A horse head! A cryptid! A monsteeer!!" Behind and to the left of Kyousuke, a female student drew back in fear, screaming.

In reality of course, it was not a real horse head, but a costume mask. And yet, it was elaborate enough to cause this timid girl to panic. Its impact was tremendous.

"The inside really stinks of rubber, too. I want to take it off already. It's suffocating meee." What's more, her voice was unnaturally high, like she had inhaled helium from a party balloon or something.

The students stared at this weird horse-person transfer student as she slowly crossed the classroom until, finally, she managed to reach the teacher's desk.

"...Phew! I'm lucky I made it this far. It's a wonder I didn't fall!"

"Yes, sorry for the trouble. Don't take it off yet! First of all, give us your self-introduction as you are."

"Okay, got it!"

After conversing with Kurumiya up on the platform, the misshapen centaur straightened herself out.

Behind Kyousuke, the same girl from before jumped and clung to the girl in front of her. "Ehh?! It l-llll-looked over heeere!!"

As for the horse person in question, taking no notice of the disturbance, she turned her face—

To stare only at Kyousuke.

"...Eh?"

Suddenly, Kyousuke had the most uncomfortable feeling. There was something *nostalgic* about this mysterious transfer student. He could *feel* it.

"Pleased to meet you everyone, and good morning. The reason why I asked to enter this school is because there's someone here I wanted to see no matter what! Even if I had to trade my life for it, I wanted to meet him, the most important person in the world to me... In order to follow after him, I got my hands on a gun! When I wasn't able to kill even one person, I felt so terrible, I just didn't know what to do... But I'm so glad I could get into this school, anyway."

"...Hey."

The effect of the helium gas must have been starting to fade—her regular voice was audible here and there behind the shrill facade. It was a voice he absolutely should not have been able to hear—

"Hey-hey-hey-hey!"

His voice trembled so much that even he found it pathetic. Shaking his head furiously, Kyousuke rejected the image that crossed his mind.

"…That's impossible." It was impossible for *her* to come to a place like this. No matter how much the voice resembled hers, or the physique resembled hers, or the presence resembled hers—there was no way such a mistake could happen…

"Yes, I'm happy…super happy! Happy, happy, happy, happy, happy, happy, happy, happy, happy, happyhappyhappyhappy, so happy I might go crazy! Ah-ha…ah-ha-ha! Ah-ha-ha-ha! Ah-ha-ha-ha-ha-ha-ha-ha-ha! Since the moment we were suddenly torn apart, the one thing that I've wished for, day after day, has finally come true! Tee-hee!"

As the false voice gradually fell away, Kyousuke's hopes crumbled. The premonition that had sprouted in his heart was already turning into a certainty. Overflowing with emotions that were impossible to process, his train of thought soon froze. It was as if the world was in a white haze.

While Kyousuke was being swallowed up by his despair, the transfer student brought her hands to the bottom of her neck.

Wait, please.

He wanted to scream, but his lips would not move.

"Ah, finally…"

His thoughts did not reach her, and the transfer student did not stop. She removed the horse head mask and cast it aside as though it were a great nuisance.

"I'm finally able to see you, *big brother!*"

The transfer student exposed her face.
Ayaka Kamiya wore a smile like a flower in bloom.

All Hope Is Gone?

CORE CRISIS

Q: What is your target rank on the final exams?
I'm dreaming big—aiming for top three in my grade!
I'm going to try like my life depends on it.

Q: What are your strongest and weakest subjects?
My strongest subject is PE, and my weakest would be any of the
classroom subjects. The exams are ALL classroom subjects, though...

Q: If you are granted parole, what do you want to do?
That's already settled, of course. I will go see Ayaka...
Wait, that answer came from my little sisteeeeeeeeer!

Q: Tell us about your enthusiasm for the tests!
No, thanks. I'm good. I actually couldn't care less...

"—And that's how it is! I'm Ayaka Kamiya, Kyousuke Kamiya's little sister. I'm thirteen years old, two years younger than my big brother. I've killed zero people, but it wasn't my fault, it was the gun's, so please don't judge me for it! By the way, the horse mask and helium gas just now were Ms. Kurumiya's idea! It wasn't my choice." With a cheerful expression, Ayaka completed her self-introduction.

"......This...can't be real!"

He felt like this was all a bad dream.

He couldn't accept the sight of his sister in this classroom.

—He *wouldn't* accept it.

But Ayaka just smiled at Kyousuke, even as he was overcome with shock.

"It's real, all right!"

She wielded the truth of the situation like a knife. "I'm the genuine article, the real Ayaka! You probably can't believe it, but I was very brave and came to see you! Hee-hee-hee! Aren't you happy? I bet you're happy. You must be happy! I'm super happy! I'm happy that I'm able to see you again, big brother! But, well...you look more rundown than the last time I saw you. Are you okay? Are you that lonesome, unable to see me?"

Kyousuke said nothing, unable to form a response.

"...Huh? Hey, hey, big brother. Why are you staying so quiet?"

"_____"

"Hey! Why are you ignoring me?! Even though I worked so hard to be reunited with you—"

"Now, now. Calm down, Miss Kamiya. You can't hurry him along like that. The surprise was clearly too much for him. You should have a little sympathy."

Luckily, Kurumiya's words seemed to pacify the hysterical girl.

"Oh, that's right! He's just sooo happy to see me that he's at a total loss for words, right? Tee-hee! That's my hopeless big brother... I love that about him, though!"

Clapping her hands together, Ayaka gave a broad smile, as if she were embarrassed. Her tone was cheerful, not the least bit different from the girl Kyousuke knew.

This isn't right.

If this was an ordinary classroom, he would understand. However, this was a classroom at Purgatorium Remedial Academy. His classmates were all murderers, and it was an extremely dangerous place. Kyousuke couldn't wrap his head around his littler sister's unwavering nerves in the face of these facts.

She should at least be afraid...

Kyousuke was surprised that he could think such things about his little sister...

Biiiiiing, boooooong,
baaaaaang, boooooong...

The hoarse chime rang, marking the passage of time.

"Do you have a boyfriend?" "I do not." "What type of boys do you like?" "My big brother." "What's your favorite food?" "Big broth—er, sweet things." "What are your hobbies?" "Making food for my main man." "What are your best dishes?" "Things that he likes. Like meat and potato stew, chop suey, and rolled cabbage." "What's your secret ingredient?" "Love (if you know what I mean)." Et cetera.

Kurumiya closed the question-and-answer session. "...Okay, that's it! I'd say you've been sufficiently introduced." Checking the time on her wristwatch, she erased the name "Ayaka Kamiya" from where it was written on the blackboard. "We're late getting started, but let's get to class now. You have exams the week after next, remember? You hurry up and take your seat, too, Miss Kamiya."

"Yes, ma'am!" Replying energetically, Ayaka stepped down from the podium. Walking with a nimble gait, she headed for the desk to the right of Kyousuke's. Its owner had been disciplined, and the seat was empty in his absence.

As if it was the most natural thing in the world, Ayaka slid into the desk with an impish grin. "Eee-hee-hee! I scored a seat next to big brother!"

"Hmm." Kurumiya nodded in satisfaction. "That will be your seat from today on, Miss Kamiya. But you may only push the desks together for the first day! Once your textbooks arrive, you'll go back to your regular spot and take class from there."

"Okaaay!"

"Don't stretch out your replies."

"Okay, I'm sorry!"

"Great."

"...Tee-hee-hee. She's strict." Ayaka stuck out her tongue. Her expression the whole time had been an unwavering smile.

Could it be that Ayaka Kamiya felt no threat either from her murderous classmates or her sadistic, violent teacher?

In this strange, twisted place, seated beside her brother, Kyousuke, the girl seemed completely and perfectly happy.

X   X   X

A chime rang out to mark the end of first period.

Before interested classmates could approach Ayaka—

"...Come here."

"Hyah?!"

—Kyousuke took her hand and forcibly led her out of the classroom. Crossing in front of Kurumiya, who was putting away her teaching materials, they drew everyone's gaze as they left the room, fully focused on heading for the hallway.

"Big brother, it's too fast—I'm telling you, it hurts! My hand hurts!"

Kyousuke ignored Ayaka's complaints.

"Goodness me, writing tests is such a pain. Even with help from my *friends*—"

"Out of the way, please."

"Whaa—?!"

Shoving aside the unappealing middle-aged man in a suit who had emerged from the neighboring first-year Class B room, Kyousuke marched them quickly up to the rooftop of the old school building. There, he finally stopped and turned to face his sister.

Rubbing the hand that had been held in his grip, she grumbled, "Big brother, geez, you're so rough... I thought my wrist was gonna be torn off!"

Kyousuke stared intensely at her. Ayaka tilted her head and blinked her eyes. "Your expression is kind of stiff. What's wrong? Are you tired?"

"_____"

Ayaka tilted her head the other way. "Huh...? Big brother? Why are you staying quiet? You've been this way the whole time! In class, you didn't respond even when I spoke to you! I don't get it!"

"...I bet."

"Eh? What did you say? You're too quiet, I can't hear—"

"I said, I *bet* you're the one who doesn't get what's going on!"

"......?!" Ayaka cowered. "Th-that's too loud..." she protested, covering her ears.

Taking one step toward his sister, who seemed oblivious to the truth of their situation, Kyousuke let it all out. The feelings that he had held inside the whole time during class, his jumbled emotions, the words that he had patiently swallowed—unable to help himself, he released them all.

"To come to a school like this...? Barging into a classroom with a shotgun? Shooting students? What have you done...? What the hell were you trying to do?! Do you understand what you did? How can you act so relaxed if you understand?! You tried to...to become a *murderer*! How can you still smile—?"

*   *   *

"Waaaaaaaaaaaaaaaaaaaaaaaaaaaaaaaaaaaaaaaaaaaaaaaaaaaaaaaa
aaaaaaaaaaaaaaaaaaaaaaaaaaaaaaaaaaaaaaaaaaaaaaaaaaaaaaaaaaaa
aaaaaaaaaaaaaaaaaaaaaaaaaaaaaaaaaaaaaahhhhhhhhhhhhhhhhhh!"

Crying in a voice loud enough to drown out her brother's angry roars, Ayaka quickly clung to him.

"But, but...I was lonely! Super, super loooneleeey! One day my big brother suddenly disappeared, leaving me all alone... I thought I would die, I was soooooo loooneleeey! Lonely and sad and bitter and hurt, with no idea at all what I should do, and every day, every day, every day every day every day every day every day every day every day every day everydayeverydayeverydayeverydayeverydayeverydayevery day I worried about yooooooooooooooooooooouuu! What could I do to get my big brother back? What could I do to see my big brother again? What could I do...? I could go to the same place as my big brother! I worried and worried and worried and worried, and thought and thought and thought and thought, and searched and searched and searched and searched and searched, and then I realized! If I did the same thing as you, I could go to the same place as you, right...? If I also committed mass murder, I would be taken to the same place as my big brother, wouldn't I? That's what I realiiiiiiiiiiiized! Because I was lonely...so lonely I could diiiiiiiieee! I wanted to see you, no matter what I had to do...ooooooooooooohhh!"

Rubbing her face against Kyousuke's chest, Ayaka ranted and raved. She wrapped her arms around him and squeezed with surprising strength, crushing the breath out of him. "When the gun didn't fire, it felt like the world was ending... I couldn't kill even one person, so I thought I wouldn't be able to go to the same place as my big brother who had killed twelve people. While I was being held down by a lot of people, I tried my best to somehow kill someone even without a weapon, but it was no good... I cried the whole time. Big brother wouldn't be coming back, I wouldn't be able to see my big brother again, I wouldn't be able to go to the same place as big brother... I kept crying for a long, loooooong time. That's why...that's why, you see? When I saw your face in that classroom, I was happy. I was super happy! No matter how scary this place is, no matter what kind of dangerous people are around, no matter how difficult an everyday life awaits me, I didn't care the slightest bit about any of that, I was so happy—"

"Ayaka…"

"I am so lucky, you see! My big brother is here! Here by my side, close enough to touch…together with me. And that's enough. Oh, I wanted to see you… I've wanted to see you for so, so long, big brother." Closing her eyes, Ayaka embraced him. Her body had become completely emaciated. Her arms and legs had been thin before, but now they were like thin sticks of wood, looking like they might shatter into pieces at the slightest touch.

What had transformed her into this state?

—It could have been nothing other than Kyousuke.

The pain of losing her brother had tormented the girl, had run her down, had gnawed away at her…until finally, the strain had caused her to go so far as to try her hand at murder.

The origin of her crime lay in Kyousuke, but despite that, he had shouted at her without giving her a chance to explain. He'd blamed her for her actions without considering the cause. He wanted to punch his earlier self.

"……I'm sorry." Apologetically, Kyousuke hugged his sister back. He squeezed gently so as not to break her skinny body.

"Big brother?" she asked in confusion.

"I'm sorry, Ayaka… I'm truly sorry for making you feel that way. Even if I apologize, it doesn't mean you can forgive me, I get that. But still, I want to apologize to you… I've wanted to apologize for a long time. Ever since the day I was arrested, this whole time…I've wanted to see you, and to apologize. I didn't imagine that you would come to see me, so I was surprised, but…now I've finally calmed down. I've also wanted to see you, just as much as you've wanted to see me. For a long, long time, I've wanted to see you."

"Big brother…" Ayaka lowered her voice in response to Kyousuke's heartfelt outpouring.

Gradually, a feeling of happiness spread through Kyousuke's chest, accompanied by the warmth of her body heat, a concrete reminder of the presence of his irreplaceable family member. "Thank goodness you didn't become a murderer…"

If by any chance the gun had fired... If Ayaka had killed people... Kyousuke didn't know how he would have felt. He was just glad that the shotgun had malfunctioned, and that Ayaka had not killed, or even injured, anybody. Kyousuke's sense of reason was still held together by that tiny shred of good news. Even so, the fact that Ayaka had even *attempted* to commit *murder* was more than enough of a shock.

Releasing his embrace, Kyousuke asked nervously, "Hey, Ayaka—don't do that kind of thing again, okay?"

"Sure!" She nodded reassuringly. "I won't. I don't have any reason to! After all, I never really wanted to do something so terrible... If it doesn't bring me closer to you, I don't want to kill anyone. I'm no murderer. Killing is scary, and I really hate it!"

"......I see."

Relieved, Kyousuke felt the tension melt from his shoulders. If that was true, then it was probably fine. What he should be doing now was not criticizing her, but soothing his emaciated little sister's heart.

Kyousuke faced Ayaka to tell her that himself. "...Of course. It's not like you would murder because you liked it."

"Tee-hee, of course not! I don't even want to get close to anyone so scary—ah!! But, you're different, big brother! Even if you are the Warehouse Butcher, who killed twelve people, I could never hate you! I'm not even scared of you! Instead, I will happily surrender my life to you." Clenching her fists, Ayaka thus tried her best to reassure him.

Kyosuke grinned at his little sister, who was always thinking of her big brother, no matter the circumstances. "Oh, thank you. I thought for sure you would want nothing to do with me if I had taken a dozen lives, but that was a pointless concern, wasn't it? That's my little sister! Gratefully allowing me to snatch away her life—nooooo, wait a minute! I haven't even killed one person!"

Suddenly leaning over her, Kyousuke frantically protested his innocence.

The fact that killing twelve people had been a false charge; the fact that, based on that false charge, he was in a deeply unpleasant situation; the fact that while at the academy he was pretending to be a murderer... Kyousuke quickly explained the whole situation to his sister.

However, he remained silent about this academy's *true character*. He thought that if he threw too much at her at once, it would only confuse her.

As she finished listening to Kyousuke's story, Ayaka replied, "In other words...you and I are the only two students at this school who haven't killed anyone, is that right? I'm so happy that we're a match, big brother! Tee-hee-hee!" She smiled broadly and embraced him again.

"Whoa!" Kyousuke was taken aback. "Geez, you... Is that the first thing you have to say? I'm happy, too, so it's fine, but..."

The figure of a certain classmate crossed Kyousuke's astonished mind. A rust-red ponytail and eyes the same color—a female student who Kyousuke knew also had a zero-kill count.

There weren't two of them, but three...

I don't have the right to reveal her secrets, do I?

Kyousuke decided to hold his tongue.

Ayaka's shoulders were trembling as she buried her face in Kyousuke's chest. She sniffed and sniffed, then let slip in a low voice:

"......You smell like a strange girl."

She was mumbling, and he couldn't hear her well.

"What did you say I smell like? Sorry if I stink like sweat... Every morning here we have something called correctional duty, you see. For nearly four hours we do physical labor. I changed out of my jersey, but surely that's...wh-what you're smelling, huh?"

"Ah, never mind! Ayaka was talking to herself just then, so don't pay any attention, please! Ayaka won't pay it any attention, either. Right, I won't worry about it, so...don't worry, yeah..."

"...Ayaka?" She had started mumbling about something, but she'd *also* said "please don't worry about it," so he wasn't going to. Right now, there was something more important to confirm first. "By the way, how did you manage to get ahold of something like a gun—"

Just as Kyousuke asked, the chime signaling the end of the break period resounded. Ayaka removed her face from his chest and looked up at Kyosuke. "Hey, big brother. This place is stricter than a regular school, isn't it...? I wonder what happens if you're late to class."

"......Ah."

He went pale before her eyes.

What would happen if they were late for the start of class?

The answer, of course, was—

X   X   X

"…Okay. I think that's enough for today. Be sure to review carefully in preparation for the end-of-term exams! Well, then, take a recess."

Kurumiya closed her textbook, gathered her belongings, and left the classroom.

Only two places on the blackboard were not completely covered with writing: a radial crack and, next to it, the fresh blood clinging stickily.

Staring at the evidence of Kurumiya's discipline, Ayaka trembled.

"C-cool…"

She trembled not with fear, but with excitement. "Miss Kurumiya is so cool! She's a powerful and gentle person, isn't she?"

"Uh, sure…that's right! Ha-ha-ha…"

Despite outwardly laughing, Kyousuke was profoundly puzzled.

After the previous break period had ended, Kyousuke and Ayaka had returned to the classroom in the middle of second period, but Kurumiya had readily pardoned them. "You must have had a lot to talk about; it can't be helped," she had said. That was the same Kurumiya who would shower students with blows for coming in just one second late.

Moreover, at the end of class, a certain someone had returned from the infirmary. "Hya-haaa! I'm back from the dead, gya-ha-ha…ah, whaaaaaat?! Who is this little brat? Don't sit in other people's seats! I'll smash—"

"Your seat is in the netherworld!! Hurry up and die so you can sit down, motherfuckeeerrr!"

"Gyaaaaaaaaaaaaaaaaaaaaaaaaaaah?!"

Fighting off Mohawk with her iron pipe, Kurumiya had protected the newbie. It wasn't impossible to understand Ayaka's feelings; her eyes were sparkling.

"If she's our homeroom teacher, it seems like we'll have nothing to worry about."

"Well, maybe? I think she was just in an unusually good mood today."

"......Kyousuke."

Just then, one of their classmates spoke to him: the female student with rust-red hair sitting to Kyousuke's left. With a look of great interest in her eyes, she glanced back and forth between Kyousuke and Ayaka, who was seated next to him on his right.

"I'd like a bit of an explanation...if you don't mind?" she asked, hesitantly.

"_____"

Ayaka's smile disappeared, and she instantly glared. But Kyousuke, who had turned to the redhead, didn't notice the change. "Huh... Oh, I didn't introduce you yet. This is my little sister—"

"I'm Ayaka Kamiya. Pleased to meet you!" Ayaka stood to introduce herself, making her way around the desk with a smile. "Are you an acquaintance of my big brother?"

With half-lidded eyes, the female student looked up at Ayaka. "...Yes. I'm Eiri Akabane. Your big brother and I sit near each other, so we get along well...to a degree. Plus, we're the same age."

"Oh, that's right! Miss Eiri Akabane, is it? Hmmm..." Having heard the female student's—Eiri's—words, Ayaka gave her a long hard look of scrutiny.

After twitching her nose several times, she mumbled, "...It's this person," and a furrow appeared across her brow.

Eiri, however, seemed to perceive Ayaka's attitude as cautiousness. Uncrossing her legs and straightening herself up, she tried to relieve the oppressive atmosphere. "...You don't need to put yourself on guard like that; there's nothing to worry about. I don't intend to cause you any harm. Of course, that goes for your big brother, too."

"—You'll keep your hands off, you say?"

"Yes, so there's no need to glare like that."

"That's right, Ayaka. Eiri looks a little dangerous at first glance, but she's really a naive and gentle person."

"Huh?!" Eiri blushed. "What do you mean by 'at first glance'?! And I'm not naive!"

"If you're not naive," Ayaka asked, "does that mean you're a bitch?"

"Wha…?" Eiri was speechless.

Ayaka stuck her tongue out impishly. "I'm joking! I don't think you're a bitch just because you look like one."

"…Tch."

"Don't click your tongue at my little sister!"

"…Why are you getting mad at me? Go die already."

"Don't tell my big brother to 'die'!"

"I said, why are you getting mad at me…?"

"Ahem, excuse me!"

From behind Eiri, who now sat sulking, another female student leaned forward.

She had short, chestnut-colored hair and wide, flaxen eyes. This girl, who was just as small as Ayaka, stood up and bowed before nervously introducing herself. "H-how do you do! I'm Mai…Maina Igarashi, fourteen years old! Just like Eiri, I am always grateful for Kyousuke's company, umm…always grateful for his company! Ah, I said the same thing twice, oh no. Ummm…"

"……Cunning."

"Ehh?!"

"Nothing. I don't think you're annoying or anything!"

"Oh, goodness! That's great if you don't think so… I'm relieved!"

"Yes, I'm relieved, too—that you're an idiot."

Kyousuke knew that Ayaka's way of speaking could sometimes be biting, but since she was smiling in a friendly fashion, there was probably no problem. *And Eiri always looks sour, so…*

"Hey, big brother. Are these girls your close friends?"

"I suppose so. They're the ones I get along with best in class."

"Hmmm…"

After looking at Eiri and Maina, Ayaka turned her face back to Kyousuke.

"Are they trying to start a fight?"

Everyone's heads turned.

"……Wha?"

"…Huh?"

"Ehh?"

"After all…" Ayaka looked around the classroom at the confused crowd. "These two are in contention for the first and second most beautiful girls in the class, aren't they? Having two girls like that all to yourself seems like it would *start fights among the boys!* If you add me into the mix, it's just going to get worse and worse! You might be killed out of jealousy, don't you think, big brother?"

"…………"

Kyousuke, who had actually almost been killed several times, was at a loss for words. On the one hand, the other students in the class—

"Hey, yeah! That's exactly right! He's got no grounds to complain, even if he's killed, I say!"

"You can't keep heaven all for yourself!! Fall into hell! Down with you!"

"Hee-hee… Everyone surround him, gang up on him and stab him, then stab the girls…hee-hee-hee."

"Huh? I don't get you. Like, no way. You can't be serious. I'm the only winner in this beauty contest, for real!"

And so on. Ayaka's words sent the class into an uproar.

Though everyone seemed immensely curious about Ayaka, nobody dared talk to her because of Kyousuke and the other girls, it seemed. The three of them, Kyousuke, Eiri, and Maina, were each for their own reasons difficult to approach, and they didn't really mingle with their classmates; they were total outsiders. The atmosphere in the classroom made that much obvious.

Ayaka whispered discreetly into Kyousuke's ear. "…Big brother, aren't you pretending to be the Warehouse Butcher here? You haven't told these people that you've never actually killed anyone?"

"……Ah." In response to this quiet question, Kyousuke nodded slightly. They, and several others, shared a secret that the other students did not know.

The true nature of Purgatorium Remedial Academy was not as a place for rehabilitating murderers. Rather, it was as an institution designed to raise them to be professional killers; their real curriculum would begin in their second year. And even once they graduated, they would not be allowed to return to honest society but would be released into the criminal underworld.

None of the first-year students were supposed to know, and that was one of the reasons that Kyousuke and the others actively avoided connecting with their peers. But most of all, this was an abnormal school where abnormal students were gathered. It was best to consider everyone, aside from the people they knew that they could trust, not as fellow students, but as *enemies*.

"Hmm…you have that much faith in them?" Ayaka stared probingly at Eiri and Maina.

"Yeah. They're reliable and trustworthy. And there are places where I can't accompany you, like the girls' locker room and girls' dorm. If anything happens, you can depend on them!"

"Oh…so in other words, my big brother has been castrated and became my big sister…is that it?"

"No! What are you saying?"

Ayaka stood, straight-faced and seeming very pleased with herself.

Kyousuke turned his gaze on Eiri and Maina, who looked rightly astonished. "I'm counting on you two," he continued. "Please help my little sister."

When he put his hands together and made his request, Eiri snorted. "…Hmph…we get it without you having to say so, geez…"

"Well, we might as well get along, then! If there's anything you don't understand, or you have any problems, pwease ask ush anytime, okay? I f-fumbled my words a bit, but…"

Kyousuke smiled at Maina. "You're fine." He was grateful for his friends' reassurances. "Thank you, both of you. And, Ayaka…"

"_____"

"…Ayaka?"

Ayaka was staring fixedly at a certain point, eyes filled with hatred. Staring at Kyousuke's hand, which was stroking Maina's head—

"Eh? Oh, sorry… What was that, big brother?"

—However, the next moment Ayaka's gentle expression had returned. She tilted her head to the side.

Eiri's and Maina's expressions turned puzzled.

…*Was it my imagination?*

"Never mind, it wasn't important…," Kyousuke said. "The point is, you also try to get along well with these two, Ayaka! Not that I would expect any problems, even if I didn't ask."

"Sure! I'll make the best of it." Smiling, Ayaka turned around to face Eiri and Maina. Her pigtails bounced and swung as she bowed. "Friends of my big brother, pleased to meet you! The two of you must have a great deal that you want to ask me, so let's spend some time chatting later, okay? Tee-hee!"

"Want to ask you? What do you mean?"

"Having to do with my brother...or not. We'll talk when he's not around."

"Concerning me...or not. Which is it...?"

Could it be a girls-only topic? I don't understand. As long as they're getting along well, I guess I don't care what kind of conversation they're having, though...

"...Sure, it's a pleasure."

"Pleased to meet you!"

Watching the three of them exchange greetings, Kyousuke felt momentarily relieved.

"Ah, there she is!" a cheerful soprano voice called out. "That girl must be the infamous transfer student, right? *Kksshh.*"

At the characteristic sound of exhaust, Kyousuke's breath stopped.

...That's right. I had completely forgotten.

There was one person left for Ayaka to meet.

X   X   X

"Oh, so you're already friends, eh?! Unfair! Let me in the mix, too!"

Gushing with jealousy, the owner of the voice marched straight toward them, crossing the classroom under a rain of inquisitive gazes. A small crowd had already gathered in the hallway, students from the classes next door hoping to catch a glimpse of the new transfer student.

"Hey, everyone! It's dear Renko Hikawa of Class B, full of energy today as always!"

She stopped in front of Kyousuke and the others. Spinning in place, she pressed an index finger to her cheek, and with a saccharine

"Ta-daa!", struck a cutesy pose. Ayaka's mouth hung open as she stared at the female student's—at Renko's face.

"Oh my! You must be charmed by my good looks, right? My beautiful face, which can make even members of my own sex fall victim to its charms, is a thing to be feared! I'm sorry, miss transfer student… I'm just too lovely! *Kksshh.*"

The boastful Renko's face was *covered by a jet-black gas mask.* It had dim plastic viewports and a cylindrical canister. Because her true face was completely hidden by the vaguely-insectoid mask, her alleged beauty, as well as any other quality about her appearance, remained entirely hypothetical.

She also wore a pair of headphones, and her appearance was, in a word, *strange.*

And while Kyousuke and the others had grown used to her, Ayaka, who was meeting her for the first time, looked shocked.

"……"

Renko tilted her head curiously at Ayaka, who had yet to even respond. "What is it, miss transfer student? Don't tell me you really are charmed—"

"Please don't talk to me."

"*Kksshh?!*"

Renko stiffened as if by electric shock.

"Your appearance is very strange, and your speech and conduct are also cryptic. Your face is hidden by a weird mask, yet you insist that you're 'beautiful'… I don't want anything to do with a freak like you."

Renko, who had been flatly rejected, flew into a panic. "Whaaaaaa—?! N-n-no way! This must be some kinda joke! Because there's no way you really said thaaat! You can't see me that way…"

"…Huh? Is it a joke, then, that thing?"

Ayaka pointed at Renko's gas mask.

"Yep. So if you don't really stick it to me, I'll think that you're funny in the head. *Kksshh*…do you understand me?"

"Uh, yes. I understand well that you are someone I don't really understand."

"I-is that so…? And I understand well that you do not understand me one bit."

Renko's shoulders slumped dejectedly.

Kyousuke scratched the back of his head, said "...Geez," and tried to mediate between the two of them. "Uh...Renko may look a little... unusual, but on the inside, she's really not all that strange! And anyway, she's my friend, just like Eiri and Maina. And she's a relatively good person, so please try to get along with her."

"......Hmph." Ayaka stuck her lip out in a pout at Kyousuke's request. "And it's another girl, too..." she complained. "Well, if you say so, big brother, I'll try, but...shouldn't you be more selective about your friends? If you ask me, a kinky chick wearing a gas mask as a joke is—"

"W-wwww-what did you saaaaaayyy?!" Renko interrupted, her voice hysterical. Ayaka drew back with a start, and Renko instantly drew that much closer, taking her by both shoulders.

"'Big brother'?! Could it be? Are...you...Kyousuke's little sister?!"

Renko, who had not heard Ayaka's introduction to the class, seemed to have finally realized that she was Kyousuke's younger sister.

Turning her face away from the gas mask as she spoke, Ayaka answered, "...Y-yes, that's right."

Renko, growing even more excited, peered down at Ayaka's face. "Now that you say it, I can see the resemblance! Something in your eyes is just like him! And there are lots of other traces, too. Yep, yep! You're his adorable little sister, all right. *Kksshh.*"

"Just a... Hey, get away from me already! Your mask is too close!"

Twisting her body around to escape from Renko, Ayaka hid behind Kyousuke.

"What is this all of a sudden?! *Ayaka* is my little sister, so what—"

"............*Ayaka?*"

Renko let forth a fierce, low-pitched sound. Her bright tone of voice was instantly transformed, tinged with threatening, dark emotions.

"......?!"

Ayaka winced at the sudden change.

Kyousuke's heart skipped a beat.

—Ayaka.

Renko absolutely could not let that name pass unchallenged. In spite of the fact that she was wearing her gas mask "safety device," Renko's bloodlust surged.

"Did you say 'Ayaka' just now? 'Ayaka'... Is that what you said?" She dropped her body low like a wild animal that had spotted prey. Her viewports reflected the fluorescent lights, shining with the glare.

"...Renko?" "Renko?" "GMK...?"

Everyone was baffled by Renko, who had caused the atmosphere to suddenly and completely change. It was the first time that they had seen her behave like this while still wearing the gas mask.

Sensing this unusual turn of events, Eiri stood up and placed a hand on Renko's shoulder. "Hold on. What's happened to you all of a sudden?"

"It's *Ayaka*."

"...Huh? Why do you know this girl's name—"

"I'm telling you, it's Ayakaaaaaa!" Renko roared, shaking off Eiri's hand. It looked like she was about to throw a temper tantrum. "Don't you know, Eiri?! This is Ayaka, A-ya-ka! The girl who is most import-ant to Kyousuke in all the world! When I confessed my love to him, Kyousuke rejected me like this... He said, 'I'm sorry, Renko. The one I love is Ayaka. That's why I can't return your feelings,' see! I lost to Ayaka...to his little sisteeer! Waaaaaahhh!"

Her sad performance concluded, Renko broke down into weeping.

"......?!"

Everyone stared incredulously at Kyousuke.

Ayaka's face was flushed bright red before their eyes. "The most important girl in all the world...? Love, me...? Rejected a...confes-sion of l-love? Eh? Eeeeeehhh?! Wh-wwwwh-what is she saying, big brother?!"

"Huh?! No, that's—" Kyousuke was utterly flustered. *Don't tell me that my sister crush is going to be exposed like this...*

Eiri and the others also began to question the lad, who was in a panic.

"Kyousuke, you...rejected a chance at love because you like your sis-ter? N-no way..."

"Ayaka is your actual little sister, though, isn't she?! That's wrong! That's totally wrong!"

"Waaaaaahhh! Stupid, stupid, Kyousuke, you're stupiiiiiiid! Picking your little sister over me, you incestuous pervert! Sister complex, sister complex, sister compleeeeeex!"

"Aaaaaargh, shut up!" Kyousuke yelled. "All of you, shut up for one secooooood!" He tried to brush off Eiri's cold glare, to cover his ears against Maina's prohibitions, to protect himself from Renko's pummeling fists.

Other voices could be heard from around the classroom and in the hallway. "Sister complex..." "Did she say 'sister complex'...?" "He's seriously ill." "Did he say he passed on GMK?!" "Mur-der-him! Mur-der-him!" "I understand his feelings... They're so nice, younger sisters..." "—No, sisters-in-law are the best!" "I've reported you to the authorities..." And things had finally, just recently, begun to calm down. Now he had drawn the spotlight again.

"Big brother!" Ayaka jumped into the dejected Kyousuke's arms. "Hey, hey, hey, hey. Big brother, do you love me? Could you possibly love me most in all the world, more than anyone else?!"

"_____"

The noisy students quieted down all at once, straining their ears to hear Kyousuke's response.

"Uh, ummm...that's, well......"

Ayaka looked up at Kyousuke, eyes brimming over with expectation.

I want to answer her, he thought. To him, Ayaka was an irreplaceable treasure. There was no falsehood in that feeling; there was only embarrassment. He didn't need to think about which feeling was greater.

"......Big brother?"

"Of course."

"Eh?"

"I love you, Ayaka! I love you most in all the world, more than anyone else! It's true, I have a sister compleeeeeeeeeeeeex!" Yelling from the bottom of his gut, he confessed his love for his sister. He had no other thoughts than *If I cheer Ayaka up even just a little by doing this, it's worth it.*

"_____"

Sudden silence.

Kyousuke timidly opened his eyes, having closed them before.

"Ooooooooooooooooooooohhh!"

Thunderous cheering broke out. The students showered applause upon Kyousuke, who had given an honest reply that he was not ashamed of. Among the excited and curious onlookers, Eiri was shocked—"...Huh?"—and Maina was shaking: "Oh dear, oh my!"

"Big brother!" Ayaka shouted, in a voice loud enough to be heard over the racket. "I love you, too! I love you most in all the world, more than anyone else! I really love you, big brother... Eee-hee-hee. I have a brother complex, so it's mutual love, isn't it!" Ayaka embraced him with all her strength.

"Th-that's right! It's mutual love, huh...ha-ha-ha!" There was no hiding the embarrassment Kyousuke felt this time around.

"......*Mutual love?*"

Renko's tears fell in heavy drops as she stood before the flirting siblings. A dark shadow had spread over her viewports, obscuring her expression...

"_____"

Clenching her fists tightly, Renko stood stock-still. The dreadful aura of jealousy rising from her body was obvious to anyone's eyes.

X   X   X

"Big brother?"

"Hm?"

"I love you!"

"Aaaaaahhh!!"

Ayaka leaped at Kyousuke, nearly causing him to drop his rice bowl. He looked down at her as she rubbed her cheek against the arm she was embracing, and he righted his "daily special garbage rice bowl" on its tray.

"Geez, you... How many times is that now?"

"Forty-three times!"

"O-oh..."

The cafeteria was crowded with murderers eating lunch. Kyousuke and Ayaka ate together, sitting close. All eyes fell on her as she kept fawning over her brother without a care.

Whispered words like "brother complex" and "sister complex" were vaguely audible, but Ayaka paid no attention. Happily clinging to Kyousuke, she said "I love you" for the forty-fourth time.

Sitting across from them, Eiri pressed against her temples. "…What good terms you two are on."

"They look more like sweethearts than siblings, don't they…?" Maina, who was sitting next to Eiri, also stared vacantly at Kyousuke and Ayaka, chopsticks dangling from her mouth.

Ayaka pulled away from Kyousuke, and puffed up with pride. "Mmhmm. That's because me and my big brother are family, and moreover we are in love! We're connected by a bond muuuuuuch stronger than sweethearts—right, big brother?"

"O-oh…"

"That's not a response! You haven't said anything else!"

"…Really?"

"Really! That was the twenty-eighth time!"

"O-oh…"

"Twenty-nine! And yet, I've only heard you say 'I love you' seven times so far… You should say 'I love you' a lot more!" Puffing her cheeks out, Ayaka glared at Kyousuke, who was trying to think of a response to his angry little sister.

"How irritating."

Renko, seated at the next table, muttered to herself, loudly enough to be easily overheard. "You think so, too, don't you, Kyousuke? At least, that's the impression that I get, hm?"

"……"

Kyousuke and Ayaka and everyone around them stopped eating and turned to look at Renko. Holding her tongue, Renko grimly accepted their silent stares as the cafeteria briefly lapsed into a strange and uneasy quiet.

"Big brother! Ignore the howling of the dog that lost the fight, and hurry up and eat!" Ayaka spoke with cheerful venom. She scooped up some of Kyousuke's "daily special garbage rice bowl" with a spoon.

"Okay, open wide!"

She held it out toward Kyousuke's lips.

"_____"

Renko's gas mask was locked on them, her blazing, ice-blue eyes almost visible.

"…What is it, big brother? My arm is getting tired." Hurrying her nervous-looking brother along, Ayaka shook the spoon.

Ayaka was growing impatient, and Renko was seething with anger. Kyousuke, stuck between the two of them, felt a sweat break out on his back as he wondered which one to favor.

"Nom."

"Yay!"

Ayaka let out a cry of victory as she thrust the spoon into his mouth.

"*Kksshh…*"

Renko, who had not been chosen, was heartbroken and dejected. The other students at her table tried to comfort her as she laid out her jelly packs and straw tube, and sluggishly prepared to eat. Anyone could see that she was sad to the point of losing her energy.

Ayaka held out a second bite to Kyousuke, who was practicing apologies to Renko in his mind. "Okay, big brother. Say 'ahh'!"

"A-again…?"

"Yep! You don't like it?"

"I don't hate it, but…"

It was really embarrassing to be fed by his little sister while everybody watched. Eiri and Maina looked at him with incredulous eyes as Kyousuke blushed, completely flustered.

"…He's a hopeless sister complex case, isn't he?"

"…A hopeless sister complex case."

The two of them sighed at the same time, and each dug into their own junk-pile lunches. This was the first opportunity for the four of them to eat together, but Ayaka was concerning herself only with Kyousuke.

—But that was probably unavoidable. This was a long-awaited family reunion—one that she had been willing to kill for. It was no surprise that she wanted to fawn over him, regardless of how it looked. Renko had called it "irritating," but Kyousuke disagreed. He was, somehow or another, happy to be adored by his little sister like this…

"Nom."

"Yay!"

Kyousuke, no longer caring what anyone else thought, swallowed another spoonful.

Ayaka laughed happily, her voice high and shrill. "Tee-hee-hee. Is it tasty? Oh, sorry…it's not tasty, is it? Garbage food like this…"

"It's good."

"Eh?"

"As long as you're the one feeding it to me, anything tastes good."

"Really?! Thank you, I'm so glad!"

"You too… Come on, now. Say 'ahh'…"

"Nom."

"Tasty?"

"Yep, tasty! Even crap is delicious when you feed it to me, big brother!"

Eiri and the others had all stopped eating and now stared intensely at the pair as they continued to intimately feed each other their meals.

"Th-this is… They're really fussing over each other, aren't they? Does she have a brother complex, or a brother-*feeding* complex?"

"Just watching them is so embarrassing I could die… Oh, dear me."

"_____"

Eiri's face spasmed, Maina blushed, and Renko stayed stiff.

Just then, Ayaka cried out, "Ah?!" "You have rice stuck to your cheek! Really, you're so much work to look after…*lick*." She removed the grain of rice stuck to Kyousuke's cheek.

"Hyah?! Hey, what are you doing?!"

"What? I got the rice off your cheek, didn't I? 'Hyah?!' you said! A cute reaction as always, hmm. Tee-hee!" Ayaka stuck out her tongue and laughed cheerfully.

"No, get it with your hand…" Kyousuke brushed his cheek.

—*Squelch.*

Renko crushed a jelly pack, splattering the lime-green, semisolid contents all over her uniform.

"My goodness. Renko, really…" The girl next to her took out a hand-kerchief and tried to wipe her clean. Slamming the table with her fist, Renko leaped to her feet.

"Gyah?!" The large girl was sent flying, the flour sack falling from her head as she toppled over. Renko ignored her completely. Throwing her jelly pack on the floor, she stormed out of the cafeteria, leaving the other students dumbfounded.

"_____"

Pausing for just a moment as she left, Renko turned and looked at Ayaka, who could feel the glaring, stabbing glint in her eyes even through the gas mask...

"Ah...big brother!" Clinging to Kyousuke's shirt, Ayaka looked up at him as he got to his feet.

"Wait here." Gently pulling her hands off him, he stroked her head. "I'm coming right back. Wait quietly with Eiri and Maina. Okay?"

"B-but..." Ayaka whined.

Leaving his sister and her objections behind, Kyousuke followed after Renko. She still had on her "safety device" gas mask; while she was wearing the device designed to suppress her vicious, violent urges, Renko didn't seem to be capable of cold-blooded murder.

Kyousuke had no idea what he would do if that should ever change. Pushing past anyone in his way, he hurried after Renko.

X   X   X

"......What the hell did you come here for?" Renko demanded, looking back at him from the landing at the top of the stairs that led up to the second floor of the old school building.

Despite the gas mask obscuring Renko's expression, Kyousuke got the feeling she was staring at him apathetically. Her voice, usually full of emotion, was quiet, and she seemed nothing like the bloodthirsty killer from earlier. "Weren't you happy getting all lovey-dovey with your darling little Ayaka back there? Why would you go out of your way to follow after me? To follow a girl you don't even love?"

"A girl I don't even love—?"

"Oh, then, you do love me?"

"Uh, th-that's..."

"...You don't love me, do you? No, you love Ayaka. If that's the case, then you should be with Ayaka. You should be with the girl who is the most important to you. You should leave me alone, since I'm not your number one, and the two of you can flirt..."

Renko clenched her fists. Her speech sounded cold and indifferent, but her hands betrayed violent emotions that she couldn't conceal. "Maybe you thought that I was gonna kill Ayaka? That I would strangle that girl to death, and soothe this irritation..."

She scolded Kyousuke, who stood, overwhelmed by her intensity. "That's why you came after me, isn't it?"

"...Uh."

"I see... It's just like I thought. You didn't come because you were worried about me. I must look like an idiot, holding out even the slightest hope...*kksshh*..." Sighing, Renko slowly descended the stairs. "...Yeah. To be sure, I want to kill Ayaka! Even though my limiter is in place, I feel like I want to kill. But you know, Kyousuke—"

After she had descended four steps, she paused. Bringing her hands close to her ears, Renko removed the headphones she always wore, and announced:

"I *can't hear* my murderous melody."

"......Huh?"

"I really want to kill her, but the tune just won't play... This is the first time this has happened to me. When I was watching you and Ayaka, so happy together, I felt so sick and angry I couldn't stand it! I wanted to cry, and scream, and rage, and smash, and kill! But I couldn't hear anything. It was so quiet, and the quiet was frightening, and I couldn't control it and I didn't understand why... I just couldn't stand it, so I had to get away..."

Groaning, Renko the Murder Maid looked distraught. Created to be a killing machine, Renko's very nature tied every emotion to the act of murder—she was driven by a powerful need to kill, and she experienced those deadly impulses as an audible melody.

The gas mask that Renko wore acted as a safety device—a limiter—designed to suppress that melody. And yet Renko felt the urge to kill even without the killer tune. She must have been confused by this new situation.

"I've killed so many people! My melody plays and commands me to do it. But now, the melody is silent. Silently telling me to kill...? No.

It's not my murderous impulses driving me to do it, it's my own genuine feelings. I want to kill."

"Renko…"

When she had first revealed her true nature to Kyousuke, Renko had told him that even without her murderous melody, she could still feel real emotions, including the desire to kill a hated rival—that was also a splendid feeling, she had explained.

"Sorry. The truth is, there's one thing I've misled you about."

"……Eh?" Renko asked.

Facing her black gas mask, he looked into her hidden eyes. "The feelings that I hold toward Ayaka are not the kind of feelings that you think. I don't love her as a member of the opposite sex, but as a family member. It's true that I think of her as the most important thing in all the world, but…you can't compare yourself to her."

"What?! But, Kyousuke, you rejected my confession—"

"Yeah. That's why, well…I'm sorry. I think I made it sound like Ayaka was the cause for that, but that's not how it is. It had absolutely nothing to do with Ayaka. Whether Ayaka existed or not, I don't think my answer would have changed."

"…If that's true, then why the hell did you make a point of rejecting me the way you did?"

"Because you misunderstood me—and it seemed like it stopped your murderous melody. And then I wasn't able to clumsily correct myself. It's not like I want to die…"

"_____"

Renko stared at the floor as Kyousuke explained.

"*Kksshh…*" A sigh escaped from her exhaust port. "Is that how it is? You recognized my misunderstanding and let it go uncorrected, then using Ayaka's existence as a shield you tried to withstand the force of my affection—is that what you're telling me?" Resuming her descent, Renko began making her way down the stairs.

"……S-sorry." Feeling guilty, Kyousuke couldn't bring himself to look at her.

"Now I see. I understand just fine. I understand what you wanted to say to me, what you wanted to apologize for. However, that's too bad—"

At that moment, Renko's demeanor changed.

"Rwaaaaaaaaahhh!!" Kicking powerfully off the stairs, she flew at Kyousuke, knocking him back across the landing.

"...Ugh?!"

Kyousuke grunted in agony as his head was smashed.

Pinning his body under her own, Renko sneered. "*Kksshh.* It's too bad, isn't it, Kyousukeee? You weren't able to withstand the force of my affection! I won't allow Ayaka, or anything else, to shield you from my feelings! Really, I'm the same as you. Whether Ayaka existed or not, my feelings wouldn't change... I would still, without fail, entrance you and kill you. So you see, there's no need to apologize."

"......Renko."

Her gloomy voice had completely changed, giving way to her usual cheery tone. "Instead, I want to thank you! I mean, even if there was a girl who was more important to you, I wasn't planning on giving up! Just, when you put on such a lovey-dovey show, I got a little taste of heartbreak. 'No matter how hard I try, I can never win,' I thought. But I was wrong. That was wrong!"

Renko, still sitting astride him, leaned down, bringing her gas mask closer. In the viewports, Kyousuke's own face was reflected. "There's no need for me to defeat that girl, is there? You don't see Ayaka as a member of the opposite sex, just as a family member. In other words, my greatest rival has disappeared without me even having to lift a hand! Now I can take you down without reserve, Kyousuke. *Kksshh.*"

"Uh, uuuh..." Kyousuke, keenly aware of the danger to his person, casually tried to change the subject. "That's right! And since we cleared up that misunderstanding, you can make peace with Ayaka—"

"No way."

"......"

His proposal was immediately shut down. Renko pulled her face away from Kyousuke's and shook her head. "Until just now, I couldn't think of anything but killing her! Getting close to someone like that would be beyond impossible. I could never do it! Even a tenderhearted maiden would have trouble!"

Renko shrugged to complete her objection.

"…I guess so," Kyousuke groaned, reluctantly prepared to give up on the idea of a relationship between the two girls.

"—Well, that's what I *want* to say, anyway."

Renko's voice was suddenly cheerful.

"Eh?" Kyousuke stared at her gas mask.

"That girl is your little sister…your family, right? She's someone who I, as your bride-to-be, really ought to become good friends with. At the very least, I want to socialize with her as members of the same family. It wouldn't do to have a strained atmosphere between a bride and her sister-in-law, now would it?"

"W-well, no…" There was a certain part of that statement that Kyousuke wanted to refute, but he obediently nodded along with Renko. Never mind a bride, he just wanted his friends and his family to get along. "Ayaka's not like me; she's not physically strong… She really is an ordinary girl, so if you stand by her, you'll be helping us both."

"Okay, leave it to me! I'm going to try to get along with her even better than Eiri and Maina!" Placing her hands on her hips and throwing out her chest, Renko was in high spirits.

"Okay. I'm counting on you, Renko! …Anyway, do you think you could get off me already?"

"No way."

"……Why not?"

"*Kksshh.*" Renko laughed seductively. "Since I went to the trouble of pushing you down, I thought I'd better make a move while we're here. When I think about you flirting with your little sister, it makes me want to make out with you, too, you know… How about it, Kyousuke? Instead of saying 'ahh' for her, you can 'uhn, uhn' with me—"

"I'll pass."

"……Why?" Renko, who was hanging over him, pulled away in evident dissatisfaction.

Kyousuke pointed at Renko's face. "…It's limp, thanks to that."

"Oh, so that's the obstacle…*kksshh.* The only thing preventing you from falling madly in love with me in my bikini on the prison camping trip was probably the mask, too, hmm… Good grief! This *is* a problem. When Mama comes back, I'll have to get her to do me a favor somehow..." Renko stroked the surface of the gas mask, grumbling to herself.

Despite her current appearance, Renko's true face was peerlessly beautiful, so she was not necessarily wrong. Kyousuke, who would be butchered the moment he fell in love with her, was grateful for the mask.

"...Well, whatever! I'll show you I can overcome a handicap like this. Love burns stronger the more that stands in its way... If a direct assault won't work, I'll have to try a careful flanking maneuver. If I can improve my relationship with your little sister, get her to like me, and then win her over to my side, you'll be that much easier to take down, won't you? *Kksshh*."

Renko let out a strange laugh. Her voice was muffled, and he couldn't hear her well, but...

"Anyway! You can relax, Kyousuke. Now that I understand that she's not my rival in love, I can become really great friends with your dear little sister. I'll call it the 'Capture Sister-In-Law AYAKA Strategy'! I'm telling you, I'm going to develop such a close relationship with her that *you'll* be jealous of *me*! *Kksshh!*"

Renko pumped her fist and spoke in high spirits. It seemed like her murderous energy had been transmuted into determination. Kyousuke felt grateful for any sense of assurance.

The Silence Is Suicide?

A DEADLY FLOWER IN EACH HAND

Q: What is your target rank on the final exams?

I don't really have a target. I'm just going to do my best work.
And I'm just going to put my bust to work for Kyousuke.

Q: What are your strongest and weakest subjects?

My best class is health class, and my worst is PE. My mask gets
in the way, and my boobs are *so* heavy...

Q: If you are granted parole, what do you want to do?

I want to go here and there with Kyousuke, and do this and
that with him.... *Mm-hmm.*

Q: Tell us about your enthusiasm for the tests!

I don't care how difficult the questions are; it'll be an
instant kill. Release on parole is within my grasp!
Kyousuke's life is in my hands, too!

"Hey, big brother. How come only the first-year students are stuck in a place like this?"

The afternoon sunlight streaming through the window cast grid-patterned shadows as Ayaka walked around the ruined first-floor hallway of the old school building. Every inch of wall was covered in graffiti.

There were three school buildings at Purgatorium Remedial Academy, two brand-new four-story buildings, and one old, crumbling, two-story structure. Of the three buildings, only the last was open to first-year students.

Kyousuke had almost never entered the new school buildings. They were the territory of the upperclassmen. "Hm? Oh, well, that's—"

"Because we're rotten oranges, you know!" Renko cheerfully interrupted Kyousuke's answer. "The first-year students aren't like the upperclassmen—we haven't been reformed yet. We'd be bad for their education. Rotten oranges turn the others bad, after all. Isolating us is a measure to prevent that."

"...I believe I asked my big brother?" Ayaka's smile disappeared, and she replaced it with a scornful glare.

"Pleeease don't be so prickly. I'm sorry about earlier, we just had a little misunderstanding is all. Can't we be friends, Ayaka baaaby?!"

"Ah, geez, don't hang on me! It's hard to walk!" Ayaka peeled Renko away and hid behind Kyousuke.

"Aww." Renko lowered her arms. "Looks like everyone hates me, huh…? *Kksshh.*"

"Well, you made a terrible first impression…but you can still patch things up!"

"……Hmph." Ayaka puffed out her cheeks as Kyousuke tried to keep Renko from falling into despair. The two of them were giving Ayaka an after-school tour of the academy. Kyousuke would have been fine showing her around on his own, but Renko had come along, hoping it would be a chance to make peace.

Ayaka appeared entirely unhappy with that fact, and sulked incessantly. "I wanted to go around with my big brother, just the two of us," she grumbled. "And anyway, what's with that getup? Is this your idea of a comedy routine? Are you trying to act like a fool?"

"Ah, finally you dug into me! Yes, yes! I borrowed this from Kurumiya, hoping it would bring us together. You like it, right?" Renko pointed to the realistic horse mask. The same horse mask that Ayaka had worn that morning was now sitting on her head. With its glossy skin and silky forelocks, and left and right glass eyes that looked in different directions—it was revolting.

Ayaka was puffing up ever larger. "I definitely do not like severed horse heads. It's not like I wanted to wear the stupid thing—geez!"

Moving nimbly, Ayaka stretched out a hand toward Renko's head.

"Wha—?! C-c-craaaaaappp!"

Despite Renko's attempt to defend herself, Ayaka stripped her of the headdress.

"Tee-hee! Too bad for you. Your real face… I will finally—" Grinning triumphantly, Ayaka leaped around in front of Renko. "…Not see it." Renko's face was, as always, covered by a jet-black gas mask.

Renko laughed theatrically, pretending to hide her face. "*Kksshh!* Too bad! I put it on top of my maaask. I foooled you, I foooled you~♪! I saw right throoough you~♪!"

"……!"

Ayaka's face was bright red. She glared at Renko, who continued mocking her triumphantly but perhaps childishly, singing, "I'm gonna tell on you!" Wordlessly, Kyousuke knocked Renko on the head with a clenched fist.

"Ow!! Kyousuke! Make love, not war!"

"That's for fooling around. I told you not to tease Ayaka."

"…Sister complex."

"Argh!"

Renko shielded her head from Kyousuke as he raised another fist.

Ayaka giggled with her usual glee and drew back behind Kyousuke. "Too bad for you! My big brother is on my side… Right, big brother?"

"Yeah, of course. I'm on your side no matter what."

"Eee-hee-hee! Big brother, I love you! I love you soooooo much!" Dropping the horse mask, Ayaka embraced her one and only.

Renko watched the girl fawn over Kyousuke, rubbing her face against his chest. "*Kksshh*…Ayaka dear, you really do love him, don't you?"

Her voice was filled with admiration.

"……Hm?" Perhaps because she found that reaction surprising, Ayaka lifted her face from her brother's chest and took a long, hard look at Renko before resuming her previous position. "Of course I do! Words can't even express how much I LOOOOOOVE him! As long as I have my big brother I don't need anything else. As long as my big brother is by my side, that's enough for me—"

"…Ayaka?"

Ayaka clung tightly to Kyousuke's body, mumbling something like an incantation as he stared down at her.

Renko, undaunted, asserted her feelings as well: "Uh-huh, I get it. I understand your feelings perfectly! Because just like you, I L-L-L-L-LOOOOOOOVE Kyousuke! *Kksshh*."

"…What?" Ayaka spoke in a low voice. Separating her body from Kyousuke's, she glared at the gas mask. "Just like me? What on earth are you saying? I'll thank you not to compare the love I have for my big brother to your nasty desires."

"It's not nasty! My love is incredibly brutal…it's heavy and intense. And it bothers me to have it compared to love that's so light and shallow and emotional. It's like the difference between death metal and pop music. My love'll blow out your eardrums and blow your mind!"

With Renko, there was also the possibility that she would literally blow your head *off*. Her love could be heavy enough to crush you, or intense enough to tear you to shreds…

However, Ayaka, who did not know about Renko's true nature, had no reason to be timid. "Oh, is that all? Really amazing…but I don't listen to death metal or things like that," Ayaka sneered. "That type of music, nothing but loud, dumb noise… I guess it's perfect for you, isn't it? Personally, I prefer approachable pop songs."

Immediately, Renko raised her voice. "Nothing but noise?! *Nothing* but noise?! *Kksshh*…looks like you don't understand a thing, Ayaka dear. Of course, even in the performance of a death growl, which, to an amateur, may sound like simple screaming, there are many subtle nuances—"

Renko launched into a fervent speech. Growls versus gutturals, screams versus screeches, sewer vocals versus drowning vocals, inhaling versus exhaling…

Eventually, after Renko had talked on and on, thoroughly covering the subject at length, Ayaka managed to get in a few words. "I don't understand one bit of what you're saying."

"Whaaaaaaaaat?!" Renko screamed in her death growl voice. She flew full speed at Ayaka like she was moshing.

"What are you doing to Ayakaaaaaa?!"

Kyousuke caught Renko with a headbutt like he was headbanging.

"Gyah!!"

Renko tumbled to the ground.

While helping Ayaka up, Kyousuke turned to her with scornful eyes. "…Geez. I thought you wanted to get along."

"Ugh…I absolutely refuse to get along with this girl! She's planning to act friendly, and then kill me when she gets the chance! She's wearing a brutal smile underneath that mask!"

"You're the one who doesn't want to get along, Ayaka… Well, whatever," Renko grumbled, brushing the dirt off her body.

Since they had already reached the exit, Kyousuke decided to continue the tour anyway. They changed from indoor slippers to outdoor shoes, and then went outside. As they toured the sprawling campus, Kyousuke showed Ayaka the gymnasium and martial arts arena, the small nature preserve called Purgatory Park, and all the other features of the school, one by one.

While he did, Renko and Ayaka were—

"Hey, hey. Do you have any sports or anything that you're especially good at, Ayaka dear?"

"I'm good at all kinds of individual sports. I'm bad at group sports, though. Like ball games."

"Oh, I'm not good at ball games, either. See, 'cause I've got heavy balls attached to my chest already."

"...Ah. They're gross if they're too big, though. Isn't that right, big brother?"

"O-oh..."

"There you go again." Renko sighed. "Even though you're always playing with my balls."

"Hang on, don't spew nonsense! Ayaka's glare hurts, you know!! In fact, she's got a dark look in her eyes...umm, Ayaka darling? What are you planning to do with that bat—?"

"Big brother, you...idiooooooooot!"

"Eeep!!"

"Your balls are dead!"

"Many animals are raised in Purgatory Park. Chickens and rabbits and—"

"And snakes like this?" Ayaka asked Renko.

"Uaaagh!! Th-thhhh-that snake is...eeeeeek!!"

"Tee-hee. Why are you screaming like that? It's pink, and I think it's lovely... Oh, are you afraid of snakes? Look, look, looooook."

"Ehh?! St-stop...don't do that! That snake contains a dangerous poison!"

"Whoops, my hand slipped."

—*Chomp.*

"Aaaaaahhh!! I-I've been biiiiiiiiiiiit!!"

"Renko?!" Kyousuke shouted. "Wait here, I'm going right now to find Mr. Busujima, and bring the antidote—"

"Don't be such a wimp, big brother! Don't you think it would be faster to suck the poison out?"

"Ehh?! No way I could, uhh…s-suck it oooooouuut!!"

At every stage of the tour, something would happen to cause an uproar. By the end, Kyousuke and Renko were exhausted and covered in wounds. They currently lay sprawled out, flat on their backs in two beds in the infirmary, where they had gone for treatment.

Ayaka alone was lively. "Hey, big brother. Are we not allowed to go see the new school buildings?" She stared at the map in her student notebook, brimming with curiosity.

Kyousuke groaned "…Unh" and tried to sit up. "No, there's no rule that says we can't go…but we would definitely be out of place. We're first-years… I think we would just stand out, and not in a good way. Give it up."

"Hmph—" Ayaka stuck her lip out in a pout. "If it's not against the rules, then let's go!" She shook Kyousuke's shoulder.

Seeing this, Renko leaped up without a moment's delay and shook him from the other side. "Yeah, yeah, let's go!" She was probably trying to foster goodwill by agreeing with Ayaka.

"Aah, okay, okay…geez, I get it." Thus Kyousuke folded, outnumbered two to one.

Ayaka shouted for joy. "Hooray!"

Renko gave a banzai cheer: "We did it, Ayaka! Yay for—"

"Well, shall we go, big brother?"

"…*Kksshh.*" Renko's banzai high five was pointedly ignored. She slowly, deliberately dropped her right hand, which had been left hanging, and followed behind Kyousuke and Ayaka, looking dejected. "Aaawww… You just wait, Ayaka baaaby! Don't forget about me!"

"…Oh, sorry. Come to think of it, what was your name again?"

"Ehh?! I'm Renko Hikawa! Although you've certainly never called me that!"

"I never have, and I never will."

"Heartless! You're heartless, little Ayaka…sob, sob…"

"Don't say 'sob, sob' with your mouth. You're not crying at all, are you?"

It seemed like it would take some time yet before these two got along.

X   X   X

"Wow...what a beautiful building! It's completely different from the first-years'."

The sparkling white school building had an elegant facade. It looked brand-new, and had been built a good distance away from the older building. Well-tended rows of trees and flowers trimmed the exterior, and not a single piece of garbage could be seen littering the walkway. Even the air seemed different from the crumbling ruin of the older building.

They came to a halt in the plaza in front of the entryway, and Kyousuke surveyed his surroundings. "...Okay. Well, then..."

"Let's go inside!"

Just as Kyousuke had turned to leave, Ayaka caught him by the collar and began dragging him toward the entrance, kicking and screaming.

"Wait, wait! You're going the wrong way!! We're not going in, we're leeeaving!"

"...Why?"

"Why...?" Repeating the question, Kyousuke looked around them. Classes has ended, and they were surrounded by students coming and going. Without exception, all eyes fell on Kyousuke and the girls. Or, more accurately, they fell on—

"*Kksshh*. We've already come this far, might as well check out the inside, too. Hey, if we just act confident, nobody will notice that we're first-years, right? Puff up your chests, your chests!" Renko's thrust her voluptuous bust forward. It bounced and shook as she spoke, looking soft.

Most of the upperclassmen who passed them stared at her breasts and face. "Hey, there's a girl over there wearing a gas mask!!" "Is she into bondage?" "Could it be a poison gas attack?" "Someone contact the Public Morals Committee!" "Her boobs are too huge!!" "What cup size are they?" "Haven't we seen that mask and those boobs before?" "I haven't." "If I had, there's no way I would forget!" "...Anyway, are they first-years?" "They must be." "Oh, they're first-years, no doubt." The upperclassmen continued murmuring among themselves.

Renko, with her gas mask and huge breasts, stood out even in the new school building. Drawing attention whether they wanted it or not, Kyousuke and the others had already been exposed as first-years.

Going inside now would be awkward, no matter what. The upper-classmen would have their eyes on them, and if they tried to start any trouble—

"Kyousuke?! Is that my darling Kyousuke?!"

A shrill, feminine, and all-too-familiar voice echoed across the plaza. The whispering of the other upperclassmen abruptly ceased, and silence descended upon the crowd. A startled Kyousuke, rigid, turned timidly to face the voice.

"Ah, it *is* Kyousuke after all! Kyousuke, Kyousuke darliiiiiiiiing!" A female student dangled out of a second-floor window, waving frantically.

"Gah?! Miss Shamaya…"

The moment she made eye contact with Kyousuke, she jumped—as if going through the building would have been too much trouble—and subsequently landed gracefully outside. She then ran toward him at full tilt. "Kyousukeeeeeeeeeeeeeeeeeeeeeeeeeeeee!"

"Guh?!"

She embraced him without slowing. "Two weeks have passed since the prison school camping trip, and I had yet to be presented with a single opportunity to see your darling face again! Oh, I was ever so loooooonely! So very loooneleeey!! And yet I never dared imagine that you would do me the honor of coming to see me! Oh-ho-ho! I'm ever so happy… Oh, Kyousuke darling! How I have pined for you, my dear-est Kyousukeeeeee!"

Rubbing her cheek against his chest, the girl was overcome with joy. She had honey-colored hair with a slight wave, and emerald-colored eyes like jewels.

This was Saki Shamaya. Kyousuke and the others had met her on the camping trip. She was their senior and a third-year student to boot.

"Just a… Calm down, please! C-calm down—"

Shamaya apparently didn't hear anything Kyousuke said. She con-tinued to embrace him. "Kyousuke, Kyousuke darling…*sniff*. What a lovely smell…*sniff*."

"Die already." A rolling savate kick smashed into Shamaya's drool-ing mouth.

"Gyaaahhh, mon Dieeeuuu!!" Shamaya collapsed, and writhed on the asphalt after taking the kick to the head.

"*Kksshh!*" Renko struck a fighting pose. "Geez, what are you doing to Kyousuke? I thought you gave up already... Looks like you really want me to take you out, Shamaya dear!"

"It's heeeeeeeeere! The monsteeeeeeeeeeeeeeeeeeer!!"

"Who are you calling a monster?! That's no way to speak to a young lady, you! Should I stab your brain in half?!"

"Eeeeeeeeek! Mon Dieeeuuuuuuuuuu!!" Nearly collapsing in fear, Shamaya drew back, clinging to a nearby student. As she trembled, a hand came to rest on her shoulder.

"Miss?"

"...Ehh? What is it?" Blinking tear-filled eyes, Shamaya lifted her face.

The owner of the voice looked down with a grin at the upperclassman clinging to her leg. "What kind of relationship is it that you have with my big brother?"

With both hands, the speaker grabbed Shamaya by the collar.

"Whaaat?!" the blonde screeched, caught off guard by the contrast between the girl's smiling face and the rough action.

The area around Ayaka's eyes twitched and spasmed as she heaved with all her strength. "I. Asked. You—What kind of relationship you have with my big brother?!"

"B-brother? My dear Kyousuke is...your big brother?! That means you are—"

"That doesn't maaaaaaaaaaaaaaaaaaaaaaaaaaaaaaaaaaaaaaaaaaatteeeeeeeeeeeeeeeeeeeeeeeeeeeeeeeeeeeeeeeerrr!!!"

Ayaka let lose a hysterical shriek, and shook Shamaya forcefully.

"P-p-p-p-p-pardon meeeeee!" Jostled violently back and forth, Shamaya apologized without understanding why.

"...Well? My big brother and you, what kind of—"

Just as Ayaka was about to again demand her answers from the girl, who was by now reeling from a concussion, Renko, who had been waiting and watching, spoke up in a serious tone. "That upperclassman, by the way, Ayaka...is a brutal serial killer who has murdered twenty-one people."

"Ehh?!" Ayaka tossed Shamaya aside, and stepped back cautiously. "Twenty-one people? Th-that many... I can't believe it."

"Yep. She has a face like she wouldn't harm a fly, but she's a *deadly maniac* who murders people as if they *are* flies. Known as the *Killer Queen*, she's a scary, scaaary murderer! Boogie-oogie-oogie!!" Renko held her shoulders and trembled theatrically.

Shamaya stared at the gas-masked girl, confused. "...Huh? Hey, you! Hiding your own nature, and so brazenly—!"

"—What's that?"

"Eeek!! Nothing at all!" The moment Renko threatened her, Shamaya curled in on herself. The terror that had been etched into her mind during the prison school camping trip apparently still lingered.

Ayaka pointed at Shamaya, who was biting her tongue in fear with a stunned expression. "...B-but she looks so ridiculously weak, though."

"It's all an act. She's a cunning trickster who will do anything it takes to kill. She's using an old trick, acting like she's very weak in order to catch her victims off guard. Most of what she says and does is fraudulent...in other words, you're better off thinking everything she does is a trap." Taking advantage of Shamaya's stunned silence, Renko said all she had to say.

Ayaka moved further away from the quivering blonde and covered her mouth with both hands. "Waaah...how wicked! What could she possibly want with my big brother—?"

"She wants to kill him."

"Eh?!"

"You see, little Ayaka," Renko began, "this girl...she was planning to mislead pure Kyousuke with clever words, seduce him, and then snatch his life away! She would suddenly embrace him as she did just now, press her boobs against him, occasionally invade his bath naked, and attack him like that... She would do as she pleased! His heart and body and life—she was planning to snatch them all away."

"_____"

The light extinguished from Ayaka's eyes as she stared at Shamaya.

"No, that was you..."

Kyousuke's jab went unnoticed.

As expected, Shamaya could not remain silent. "Now you wait just a moment!" She interjected. "I absolutely shall not stay quiet and have you carry on as you please…" Glaring at Renko, she got to her feet and stepped in front of Ayaka.

There, Shamaya's expression shifted from a devil's anger to an angelic smile. "My darling Kyousuke's younger sister… May I address you as such? Miss Hikawa's words are nothing more than irresponsible nonsense. You must not take them seriously—they are unfounded lies."

"…Lies."

"Yes, they are all lies! From the bottom of my heart, I love Kyousuke—"

"Liiiiiiiiiiiiiiieeeeeeeeeeeees!" Ayaka screamed, pushing Shamaya away.

"My word!"

Shamaya tumbled over.

"Did you think that you could fool Ayaka, Miss?" the girl continued coldly. "Saying that you love my big brother… Don't run your mouth so thoughtlessly! Ayaka is disgusted."

"That's right, that's right! There are some things that you can say, and some you cannot!" Renko piled on, condemning Shamaya.

"Whaaat?!" Shamaya straightened up, facing both of them. "Why are you attacking me like this?!"

"Because you touched big brother."

"Because you embraced Kyousuke, of course."

"Ehh?! Just for that—"

"'Just that'?!" Renko's and Ayaka's voices shrieked together.

"I told you, didn't I, Ayaka? This girl thinks nothing of embracing a member of the opposite sex. Seems she's accustomed to close physical relationships. She's an unimaginable tart."

"She is, she is. She has no understanding of how valuable a hug with Ayaka's big brother is, does she?! It's like pearls before swine, or gold before a homewrecking cat! What a tart."

Shamaya, being abused by both of them, flushed red and tried to retort. "I…I am not a tart! I am still pure! I have no personal experience with XX or XX or XXX or XXXX, and XXX and XX and XXXX are still no more than wild ideas! Every night, I do XXX and XXXX for my darling Kyousuke, but that is part of being the lady he loves. And sooner or later, I will actually… Heh-heh-heh…"

"Wh-whaaa…?" Ayaka and Renko were both stunned.

"Why are you backing away?!"

"S-sorry…that's pretty seriously revolting."

"The 'heh-heh-heh' was especially bad. That's not a face a lady should make."

"Well, I never!" Shamaya threw her head back in shock. Crumbling weakly, she asked herself, "Am I revolting?"

"Yes. You're gross."

"Yep. Gross!"

"Whaaattt?!"

The girls showed no mercy.

Shamaya went white. She looked too pitiful.

"…Hey. You two have gone too far! Drop it." Kyousuke muscled in between them.

"Kyousuke dear…" Shamaya's eyes sparkled as Kyousuke extended a hand to her—

"Eeek!"

—But as she tried to stand, Ayaka attacked Shamaya from the side, breaking her grip on Kyousuke.

Losing her support, Shamaya tumbled over. "Gyah—oh my!!"

"Ow… Hey, what are you doing?!" Kyousuke snapped, shocked.

Ayaka raised her elegant eyebrows. "Ayaka should ask you the same thing, big brother. What are you doing?! Helping this girl—?!"

"Now, now, Ayaka dear." Renko stepped in to pacify her. "Kyousuke is too kind, so he helps everyone without thinking. He's a pure soul, so he's easily fooled by deception… He thinks too highly of others and can't tell them that their disagreeable traits are disagreeable. She's just taking advantage of Kyousuke's good nature."

"No way," Kyousuke replied. And then: "You must really hate Miss Shamaya."

"Oh, so you like her, Kyousuke?" Ayaka asked.

"Uh…" Kyousuke didn't answer.

Just as Shamaya had nearly been killed by Renko, Kyousuke and the others could also be killed at any time by Shamaya. However, since Shamaya, unlike Renko, did not have a limiter equipped, it wouldn't be clear whether she was trying to kill them again. Kyousuke didn't like her, so much as fear her.

"Look, he can't even give a reply! There's your answer, Ayaka dear. *Kksshh.*"

"I see. I understand perfectly well. She follows him around even though he really doesn't like her and finds her annoying... Poor big brother. Taking advantage of his kindness to try to capture his attention... This upperclassman is the worst! Please don't come near us ever again."

"Eh? You two, wait a—"

"Big brother, she's a serial killer who murdered twenty-one people! I'm worried about you... I'm worried about your life! But you just ignore my feelings... Ignore me and make friends with this murdering upperclassman?! How cruel."

"...Um." Kyousuke faltered under Ayaka's tearful gaze. When he looked around for an escape route, he saw Shamaya staring right at him.

"Kyousuke darling? What she said...about you hating me... It's a lie...isn't it?"

Her tone of voice and facial expression were blank and lifeless.

Kyousuke found that alarming. He spoke carefully, sure he was inviting trouble. "Ah, well...to be honest, hate is—"

"Waaaaaaaaaaaaaaaaaaaaaaaaaaaaaaaaaaaaaaaaaaaaaaaaaaaaaaaaaaaa ahhh, noooooooooooooooooooooooooooooooooooo!"

—is not the right word!

Before he could finish speaking, Shamaya leaped up and ran away, leaving Kyousuke and the others behind. Trailing tears, in the blink of an eye she had faded away into the distance.

"The Killer Queen brought to tears by...a first-year boy?"

One of the upperclassmen watching the scene muttered in surprise. The silence that had descended upon them broke, and the plaza filled with commotion.

"Miss Shamaya is...u-unbelievable. I mean, what is their relationship?!"

"Were the rumors true? That Saki's fallen in love with a first-year..."

"Stuuupid!! She's everyone's idol... She's our Madonnaaaaaa!"

"Her fan club won't stand by, either! They're all gonna die!"

"I'll go get a Tokarev pistol." "I'll get an AK-47." "I shall fetch my katana." "I'll bring an iron maiden." "Let's sort it out before the teachers get here." "Okay, when will we kill them?" "Now!"

"Ruuuuuuuuuuuuun!"

As he shouted, Kyousuke grabbed Ayaka's hand and ran with all his strength.

"Wah! Big brother, you're fast—"

"Ayaka, hurry! If they catch us, we'll be killed!!"

Following behind Kyousuke and the others, a crowd of upperclassmen gave chase in a fit of rage. Their eyes were filled with anger, and many of them carried weapons. As Renko had said, if the mob caught up with them, they would not fail to take their revenge.

Their after-school period had turned into a game of very high-stakes tag.

X   X   X

"Damn, they sure can run fast... Where the hell did they go?! I'll fill 'em with holes!"

"Free time's gonna end. We won't have time to torture 'em right?!"

"Hya-haaaaaa! Where oh where oh where are you, ya bastards?! I'm cooomiiing!"

"Whoa! W-watch out—Was that a modified motorcycle just now? Hella old-school..."

"Hey, you asshooole, you! Worthless Mohawk! Don't ride my precious bike arooouuund!"

"Huh...it's Loli-miya! Everyone, drop your weapons and run!! If she finds them we're screwed!"

"Whaaat?!" she roared in an angry bellow. "Which one of you pigs just squealed 'Loli'? Do you want me to smash you up?!"

"......"

The tumult faded away. They all kept still, holding their breaths for a long while, until they couldn't hear anything. It seemed the upperclassmen had all been chased off by Kurumiya's rampage.

"...Do you think it's okay now, big brother?"

"Yeah, probably. Let's get out of here before they come back—*cough, cough.*"

"Ahh?! Kyo-Kyousuke...where are you touching?! Don't do that, that's where..."

"Big brotheeeeeeeeeeeeeeeeeeeeeeeeeeeeeeeeeeeeerrr?!"

"Just a... Don't get violent, Ayaka! The ash is—*cough, cough, cough.*"

Unable to stand it any longer, Kyousuke pried open the lid. They burst free into the open air, rolling out into a square of light. Kyousuke and Ayaka both were covered in white from the tops of their heads to the tips of their toes.

"Heave-ho!" Following after the desperately choking siblings, Renko, her whole body white just like the other two, casually wormed her way out. "You two look like you're having a hard time. Did the ashes get in your lungs, I wonder? Just kidding!"

"Ugh. No fair, you have a gas mask...*cough, cough.*" Ayaka, teary-eyed from too much violent coughing, glared at Renko bitterly.

Renko laughed, "*Kksshh,*" and brushed off her ash-covered clothes. "Your thrashing only made it worse, Ayaka! Inside an incinerator, you have to stay still."

"Excuse me! Whose fault was it that I was—*cough, cough.* Uuugh!"

"It was dark and cramped, in there, all right? It's not my fault, either. A few mishaps were bound to happen, Ayaka dear." Renko patted Ayaka's back to soothe her coughing fit.

When their breathing finally settled, Kyousuke and his sister brushed the ashes off each other.

"But it was a bright idea to hide inside the incinerator, wasn't it?" Renko said.

"Yep, yep. Very clever! We escaped death—narrowly—thanks to that," Kyousuke replied.

"Eee-hee-hee." Ayaka beamed. "I don't have any stamina, so I thought I would be caught in that game of tag...but I'm confident in my hide-and-seek abilities! But...how come there's so much ash?"

"Um. Th-that's because..."

Because the incinerators are used for more than just garbage...

That was the rumor, but he thought it would frighten her, so he held his tongue. *Surely* they must have imagined those long, narrow, white shapes buried in the ashes...

"*Kksshh*...well, then. Now that we've got the mess off, let's get moving before we're found out."

"Right, we should hurry back!" Kyousuke announced. "Even those guys probably won't come as far as the old school building..."

"I hope you're right, but they probably hate the thought of giving up!"

"I just wish I could catch that upper-crust tart alone," Ayaka muttered. "Her followers seem really persistent, though."

"Yeah, yeah. It stinks of bitch to conveniently manipulate them like that," Renko agreed.

"Stinky, stinkyyy! Tee-hee."

"...You two have no remorse, do you?"

Along the way back to the old school building, Ayaka and Renko worked themselves up over the topic of Shamaya. The content of the conversation was a little questionable, but—they had made a common enemy in Shamaya, and by cooperating to escape from the juniors and seniors, the gulf between the two girls had naturally closed. Kyousuke was happy to see the two of them talking harmoniously, though he couldn't help but feel a little sorry for Shamaya. He would have to try to work things out and get them to apologize later.

"Hey, Kyousuke. Free time is going to end soon, you know?" Renko pointed to the campus clock.

"...Yeah." It was 5:39 PM. Free time after classes ended when the evening's manual labor started at 6:00 PM. The students were expected to assemble, change into their tracksuits, and be ready to work, no later than five minutes to 6:00. "Is it already that late? We don't want to be tardy, so let's head to the locker rooms—"

Breaking off midsentence, he suddenly remembered that, because it was exam week, correctional duty had been canceled, starting this afternoon. Instead, all students were obligated to return to their dorm rooms no later than 6:00 PM to study. "...No, let's go back to the dorms."

Thankfully, since they had left their bags in the student dorms, there was no need to stop by the classroom. All the upperclassmen seemed to have gone back to their area, too, so all that was left was to leisurely make their way back.

Renko stretched—"*kksshh*"—and both her abundant breasts and her cheerful voice bounced vigorously. "Wooow, it's so great not to have to do any manual labor! This mask is really suffocating, and it kills my field of vision, so I suffer no matter what I'm doing."

"Then wouldn't it be all right to take it off...? It's a pretty good gag, even if you don't carry it any further. Are you a comedian? Or is your bare face just that ugly?" Looking at Renko's gas mask, Ayaka tilted her head. As usual, she had struck hard, likely because she was still wary of her tentative ally.

However, Renko did not seem upset, and wagged her finger. "*Tsk, tsk, tsk.* Quite the opposite, my little Ayaka."

"...Meaning?"

"My real face is too beautiful, so I'm deliberately concealing it!"

"...Ah, okay, sure. You're joking."

"No. It's not a joke, it's the truth. It's not that I won't take my mask off—I can't take it off. No matter how inconvenient or sweltering it might get. Do you know why that is?"

"Hey, Renko! That topic is—"

With the palm of her hand, Renko stifled Kyousuke's interruption.

If they touched on the subject of the gas mask, they would not be able to avoid disclosing Renko's true nature. It was an overwhelming topic to discuss, especially now that Ayaka had finally begun to open up to her. The distance that they had tried so hard to close would surely widen again, and it would place a needless burden on Ayaka's mind.

However, Renko spoke without hesitation:

"The reason why I cannot take off this mask: It is because my bare face is too dangerous."

"...Huh?"

"*Kksshh.*" Renko sighed at the siblings, a pair of gaping mouths.

Stroking the exterior of the gas mask, she turned her head to face the setting sun. "There's such a thing as a femme fatale, isn't there? That's how my good looks go. I seduce people's hearts and drive them crazy. The people who have had their hearts stolen by me would need to steal something of mine in return, and we would both snatch away each others' lives...so, I cannot remove my mask. I could not bear to see people get hurt on my account. Oh...I'm, I'm—"

"......Pff."

Renko looked at Ayaka. "Hm?"

Ayaka had stopped walking, and now stood doubled over, her shoulders trembling. Then, as if she had reached the limit of her endurance, she exploded into laughter. "Ah-ha-ha-ha-ha-ha-ha-ha-ha-ha! Wh-what was that…? You're so funny! That was from the narcissist school of acting, was it? Hee-hee…okay, I get it, you're a real beauty! Though it's a one-in-a-million chance that that's true. Ah-ha-ha! You really are a weird one!"

Renko stood, looking perplexed. "Ummm…I feel a little bit like you're making fun of me!"

Ayaka wiped away at tears welling up in the corners of her eyes. "It's because you sounded so stuuuuuupid!! Really, a femme fatale?!" She continued laughing loudly.

Just when the conversation was getting too serious—that's Renko's style all right! Kyousuke felt like it was the first time since coming to the academy that Ayaka had shown anyone else her *true* smile. "…Thank you, Renko."

"Hm?"

"Nothing…" Kyousuke turned away from his buxom classmate, who tilted her head in confusion. Embarrassed by the gratitude he had unconsciously expressed, he had a strange feeling in his chest. *This emotion is warm and ticklish—*

"Big brother!"

The feeling disappeared as Ayaka vigorously clung to him. She wrapped both arms around Kyousuke's chest and smiled. "Tomorrow and the next day are school holidays, aren't they? What do you want to do to spend time with me?"

"…Hm? Oh right, tomorrow's Saturday…"

Purgatorium Remedial Academy followed a five-day weekly schedule. Students could choose from a number of various ways to spend the weekends when classes were not in session.

They could play sports on the school grounds, or read in their own rooms, or diligently work out, or stuff themselves in the cafeteria, or practice on instruments in the music room, or spend the whole day asleep in bed…

While restricted to school spaces, the students could make the most

of their plentiful leisure time. However, this proved to be surprisingly difficult. Kyousuke and the other students, faced with time to kill, were always getting into trouble.

Faster than Kyousuke could answer, Renko suggested, "We have exams really soon, so let's hold a study party with everyone!" She jumped at him from the side opposite Ayaka and grabbed hold of his arm in the same way. Kyousuke's left arm slipped in between her abundant breasts and was buried.

"Huh?! Hang on, just what are you doing, taking advantage of him like that?!" Ayaka let go of Kyousuke's arm long enough to tear Renko loose. Her eyes burned with hostility. "Stop squishing those things against my dear big brother!"

Her smile, which had been there until just a moment ago, was nowhere to be seen, and her mood had deteriorated instantly.

Heaving up her breasts, Renko sighed. "*Kksshh*...do my boobs really bother you that much, Ayaka baby?"

"No! *You're* what's bothering me!"

"Ehh?! And I thought we'd become friends..."

Ayaka stuck out her tongue at the crestfallen Renko with a "Bleh!" She held tight to the arm that Renko had grabbed, as if to reclaim it as her own. "You got carried away and got too close! It doesn't matter how much of a fuss you make, please don't touch him so casually. It's way too familiar! Or are you a tart, too?"

"I'm not a tart—I'm a niche!"

"Yes, yes, that's right. Girls wearing gas masks and stuff like that aren't really in demand everywhere, are they? Of course, they're mysterious...but I will not give my big brother to someone inscrutable like you! Absolutely no way will I ever give him over!" Ayaka squeezed tighter, emphasizing her determination.

Renko hung her head. "You're a formidable sister-in-law, huh..." However, she promptly had her energy back: "But I'm not discouraged! If pushing is forbidden, I'll pull, and if I can't play it straight, I'll play the fool. In order to open up your heart, first I have to open up my legs!"

"Once you open them, what then?"

"Wasn't that sour..." Without missing a beat, Renko turned the joke around. Kyousuke was stunned. The strength visibly went out of Ayaka's arms. "*Kksshh*. Well, that's how it is, so let's do our best! I don't know what you think, Ayaka, but I want us to become good friends! Come on, let's go together!" Renko extended a hand toward Ayaka.

There was a fork in the road right ahead of them. To the right was the girls' dorms, and the left continued on to the boys' dorms. The dorms of the opposite sex were strictly off limits, so Kyousuke would have to separate from the two of them there. Ayaka trembled and squeezed his arm ever tighter.

"Big brother…"

"It's okay. Renko is my friend. You're not going to be snatched away and eaten."

"Yeah. I'm exceedingly normal, you know. I don't attack and eat girls or anything."

"…Do you attack and eat boys?"

Renko laughed—"*kksshh*"—and did not answer further.

Ayaka sighed, and let go of Kyousuke's arm. "Well fine. There are all kinds of things I want to ask Miss Mask anyway…"

"Things you want to ask? Well, my cup size is G…"

"…Big brother." Letting Renko's response slide, Ayaka fixed her gaze on Kyousuke. Her dark eyes wavered anxiously, like the surface of the water at night. "I'm going to see you again soon, right? I can see you the day after tomorrow, and the day after that, right?"

"Yes, of course. I'll be waiting for you right here every morning." Nodding, he stroked her head.

Ayaka narrowed her eyes like she was embarrassed. "…Okay, I understand. In that case, it's all right." Smiling, she walked over to Renko, ignoring her extended hand as a matter of course. "See you tomorrow, big brother! Don't you dare skip out on studying for the tests!"

"I know, I know… You try to get along with everyone, okay? And—" He turned to look at Renko, who had withdrawn her hand dejectedly. "I'm entrusting Ayaka to you! Together with Eiri and Maina, help her out with everything."

So saying, he finished with a bow.

Renko's sighs gave way to high spirits as she sprang back. "*Kksshh!* Leave it to me, Kyousuke! There's no need to get Eiri's and Maina's help…as long as I, Renko, am in this world, no one will be allowed to lay a finger on dear Ayaka!"

"You're not allowed to lay a finger on her, either, you know."

"Wh-wh-what are you saying?! Hyah!!" Renko thrust her fingers toward Ayaka.

"Oh, too baaad," Ayaka teased as she dodged Renko's attack. "You missed! Tee-hee!"

Kyousuke smiled wryly, and pointed to the fork in the road ahead. "Well, I'll be going, then. Don't fight too much, okay, you two?"

"Okay, good night! You don't have to worry, we won't fight."

"Good night, big brother! Let's spend all of tomorrow together, just the two of us, okay?"

"Objection! You can't hog him, Ayaka! Tomorrow we'll have a study party with everybody—"

"No we won't."

"What did you saaayyy?! Outside with you, brother complex!"

"I am outside, though. Don't say stupid stuff, let's get going already!"

"Ah, okay."

"…I take back what I said. I'm entrusting Renko to you, okay?"

With Ayaka in the lead, they headed off toward the girls' dorms.

Please, don't let any trouble happen while I'm not around… Wishing hard, Kyousuke started down the path toward the boys' dorms.

X   X   X

"……Hmph."

Gripping a mechanical pencil, Ayaka puffed out her cheeks.

Saturday morning—the next morning—saw Ayaka in a foul mood.

"But I wanted to spend time alone with my big brother, especially now…"

"Now, now," Renko pacified the grumbling girl. "Isn't this nice? Surely we'll all make more progress studying together! *Kksshh.*"

"She's right, she's right! If two beds are better than one, then five must be even greater! There's no problem we can't solve!"

"I think you mean 'two heads are better than one'…unless you think the answers are going to come to you in your dreams!"

Maina enthusiastically waved her pencil as Kyousuke poked fun at her.

"…*Fwah.*" Eiri, meanwhile, let out a yawn.

"Grrr…" Ayaka ground her teeth. "We won't make any progress like this!" she shouted, pointing sternly at Renko, Eiri, and Maina. "In fact, we're making the opposite of progress. You're all deadweight! Anchors A, B, and C!"

"Come on." Kyousuke made her lower her pen. "Didn't you all get a little friendly in the dorms...?"

"No way!"

"Yep!"

"Would have been nice."

"Not yet..."

"Your answers are all different..."

This had started an hour earlier. Early that morning, Kyousuke had joined up with Ayaka and they had gone to an open classroom to study for the tests. They had talked about the girls' dorms—about how her room appeared to be a single-occupancy cell, about how the bed was so uncomfortable, about how the jailers were neurotic and bothersome, about how she had bathed with Eiri and Maina, about how Renko did not remove her mask even in the dorms, and so on. Ayaka had told him all of this while they studied.

The morning had been a success up to that point. But then, less than an hour after Kyousuke and Ayaka had begun their study session, Renko and the others had appeared with materials in hand and joined in. As a result...

"...Hmph." Ayaka was sulking, tearing her eraser to pieces.

Kyousuke and the others each had their study materials spread out over an island made of four desks pushed together. Kyousuke and Ayaka were next to each other, and across from them sat Renko and Maina, respectively. Eiri alone was at her own separate desk, elbows propped up on it in boredom.

"Your manners are poor, Miss Washboard."

"I don't want to hear anything from you."

The "Miss Washboard" to whom Ayaka had referred was, of course, Eiri. Ayaka had apparently given her the nickname in the bath the night before.

"*Kksshh*... Don't tell me a girl two years younger than you is more developed?"

"...I meant about manners!" With her elbows still on the desk, Eiri nodded at what Ayaka's hands were doing.

Dropping the torn and crumbled eraser, Ayaka laughed. "Tee-hee! Miss Washboard, you're totally flat, aren't you? I could have mistaken you for a boy or something."

"...What did you say?"

"H-hey...quit it, Ayaka! Boobs are a sore subject for Eiri..."

"Oh, so she's sensitive about it? I found Miss Washboard's soft spot!"

"Come to think of it, aren't you even flatter, Ayaka? I know you're still thirteen, but still—you don't have any curves at all! You're not much different from Eiri..." Maina chimed in.

"You're being annoying, Crafty Cat! Saying you look great with your clothes off is too cunning." Ayaka threw a fragment of eraser at Maina.

The "crafty" in Crafty Cat referred to Maina's "cunning," and adding "cat" to the end was a way to make it sound cute. It was a mean nickname, like calling Eiri Miss Washboard.

"Oh, goodness me, I'm sorry, Ayaka... I look smaller than I really am when I'm dressed."

Even in low spirits, Maina maintained a somewhat cheerful demeanor. She clearly didn't understand the origin of the nickname, though she seemed happy with the idea.

"Oh, wow...how nice! I wanted to get in the bath with everyone, too. And then I would have been able to show off my bodacious body to my heart's content. *Kksshh...*"

"Your *audacious* body isn't important, Miss Mask," Ayaka snipped. "I'm way more interested in seeing your bare face. You've got to take the gask mask off when you have a bath, right?"

"*Kksshh.* Of course not. I leave it on even when I take a bath."

"Liar," Kyousuke teased. "You took it off, diiiiiidn't you?"

"......?!"

Everyone turned to look at Kyousuke all at once, eyes and mouths open wide in surprise—and anger.

"...Huh? She 'took it off'? What do you...? Don't tell me you peeped on the girls' baths—"

"Immoral! Shameless! Criminaaaaaal! I misjudged you..."

"Hey, big brother...there's something I want you to tell me that's more important than studying!"

Eiri was surprised, Maina was disappointed, and Ayaka had her mechanical pencil ready. Kyousuke finally realized his slip of the tongue.

"Ah?! Wait, that's not it! What I said just now, that's not what I meant—"

"We got in the bath together."

"Yeah, yeah, that's right! I had gotten in the bath alone, when she barged in and pressed her naked chest on...never mind!"

It wouldn't be wise to share that experience. Kyousuke suddenly found himself drenched in sweat.

Ayaka thrust the tip of her pencil toward his left eye. So that he couldn't escape, she held the back of his head with her opposite hand. "...What are you talking about, big brother?"

Click. With a smile, she extended the thin shaft of graphite.

"A-Ayaka...? Um, I'm afraid for my eye, so—"

"I want you to answer me quickly. Come on, quickly! If not..."

Click. Still smiling, she extended the graphite again, inching it closer to his eyeball.

"Hey, wait, joke...it's a joke, Ayaka! A f-figure of speech—"

"Oh, really? If you're lying, Ayaka...will get angry!"

Click, click. Her smile disappeared. The black needlelike tip was just millimeters away.

"......"

Ayaka's eyes were peaceful, like the surface of calm water, but beneath them lurked a shadow of rage that seemed ready to explode at any moment. Gulping loudly with a dry throat, Kyousuke was about to open his mouth, when—

"Just kiddiiing!"

—A fingertip thrust between them broke the graphite shaft off at the base. "Of course it's not true. As difficult as it is to get into the opposite sex dorms, there's no way to peek into the bath. Getting in together would be entirely out of the question! It would be impossible." Placing both hands on the desk and leaning forward, Renko flatly denied the whole affair.

Kyousuke, who didn't want anyone to know the truth, followed her lead immediately. "Yeah, yeah, entirely out of the question! It was a joke. Don't take it seriously...ha-ha-ha..."

"Hrrrm." Ayaka scrutinized the two of them suspiciously.

"What? Of course it was a joke!!"

"...It's okay, I was joking, too." Ayaka flashed them a broad smile and abruptly released Kyousuke, lowering the mechanical pencil.

"*Kksshh...*" Renko also sat back down. The uproar seemed over—for now.

"...Geez. Even if you were joking, you went too far, Ayaka! Your pencil is not meant for stabbing eyeballs. It's for writing. I thought you were really going to do me in, geez..."

"Yep. If it had been true, I was planning to push it in just like this!"

"Uh..."

"It's a joke, I said! Tee-hee!"

"......"

A bad joke.

Kyousuke grimaced. Ayaka leaned her shoulder against him, peering at their spread-out problem sheets and notebooks. "Never mind all that. Let's get to studying, big brother. You don't want to get failing marks, right?"

"...Yeah." They had gathered today to study, after all. They couldn't just get caught up chatting all day.

The Purgatorium Remedial Academy tests were not examinations so much as *death*inations. The thin red line separating life and death was drawn at "less than half of the average score," which was a worrisome situation. Any student who wanted to avoid Kurumiya's discipline was sure to be studying as if their life depended on it. If everyone studied, the average score would be high, and if the average score was high, there would be more room for failure. To make matters worse, Kurumiya was the one in charge of the tests. They had no way of knowing what kind of cruel trick questions might appear.

Coming back to his senses, Kyousuke took up his pencil. "...The tests cover a lot, so we'd better start taking this seriously."

"Right." Ayaka nodded. "If there's anything you don't understand, just ask! I can teach you."

"Teach us? You? Did you forget that you just transferred in?"

"Of course!" Ayaka answered, sticking out her chest. "The classes at this school are middle school level, right? Then it's no problem for me. The material might be different, but the main points are the same. Besides, it looks like it's mostly review."

"Oh, yeah...?"

Purgatorium Remedial Academy followed the compulsory middle school curriculum. Since the ages of the students varied, the material was geared toward the lowest levels, but there were many students who had completed their schooling in the outside world, and these would be the first big exams since the semester had started.

Ayaka smiled sweetly at Kyousuke, who looked satisfied with her answer. "So, big brother. Why don't you aim to rank in the top three of our year, along with me?"

What an outrageous goal!

Kyousuke was about to ask "Why would you try for such a thing?!"— but he quickly reached his own conclusion. The top three students of their year would be granted off-campus parole. Without the desire to see Ayaka motivating him, Kyousuke had lost any ambition to score well, but...

"If we're both granted parole together, *we can go on a date!* We can sing karaoke, or go to an amusement park, or go shopping. We can go wherever we like, all to our hearts' content!"

".....?!"

Renko, who had been moving her pencil in time with the music leaking from her headphones, froze. Maina, who had been staring at her problem sheet, snapped her head up. Eiri stifled a yawn. Grumbling leaked from each of their three mouths, respectively.

"...Karaoke."

"...An amusement park."

"...Shopping."

Kyousuke's vague reply resounded through the almost-silent classroom. "Well, that sure sounds good, but not enough to work like my life depends on it... The hurdle for getting into the top three in our year is extremely high for me, not to mention you, Ayaka!"

The difference in his motivation level between when he first heard about the tests and now was about the same as the difference between heaven and earth. Kyousuke had a mind to give up before the tests even started.

Ayaka encouraged him, "I told you, I'm going to help you! With that attitude, you can forget about top three—you're in danger of failing!! Don't you want to go on a date with me, big brother?"

"Well, uhhh…"

"I'll teach you!" Renko thrust her body forward as Kyousuke struggled to answer. She brought her gas mask near to his face, and raised her voice over the loud sounds of exhaust. "*Kksshh!* I might act dumb, but I have confidence in my IQ. There's no reason why you can't make it into the top three! What do you want me to teach you first? Math? English? Or maybe…physical education? *Oh yeah!*"

"Don't say 'oh yeah' like that. And anyway, I'm going to get Ayaka to teach me, so I don't need you."

"Ehh?! You're going to learn physical education from your own actual little sister?!"

"Geez, come on, you're in the way!" Ayaka shouted, pushing Renko's face aside forcefully. "Back off, Miss Mask!"

But Renko did not give up, and circled around Kyousuke, dragging a chair. "*Kksshh.* Ah, you're stuck on this problem, are you? This is—" Sitting next to Kyousuke on his right, she tried explaining it to him.

Ayaka's face turned bright red and she stood up, moving to pull Renko away from him. "Come oooooon! I'm going to teach my big brother, I toooooold you! Give my brother baaaack! Give him back, give him baaaaaack!"

While Ayaka stood shouting, Maina finished the headband she had been making. On the white cloth, in black permanent marker, was written RELEASED ON PAROLE in big letters.

Eyes full of determination, Maina squared off against the problem sheet. "Top three in the class… It's probably foolish for someone dumb like me to even try. But still, I'm going to do my best! Because Kyousuke told me to 'follow my feelings'… I won't give up! I'll try with all my might and aim for being released on parole!" Maina waved her pencil fiercely. The classroom had grown quite noisy.

Giving the tumult a sidelong glance, Eiri spoke from her separate, single seat. "…Getting released out on parole isn't worth worrying about. Are you stupid?"

Not determined at all, she yawned slightly. Rather than taking up a pencil, she had started on a pedicure, and was already busy painting her toenails.

✕   ✕   ✕

"Oh, your calculations are wrong again! Look here, and here. The way to solve it is right there, but it's no use…you're not careful enough in the final step, big brother."

"From now on, we need to check all your work, okay? If you're aiming for the top three, I think carelessness could be your fatal mistake."

On his left, Ayaka was checking his answers, while on his right, Renko was giving him advice. Two hours had passed since the start of their study party. Kyousuke had thought that with all the chatting their studies would go nowhere, but they were progressing surprisingly well.

Even Renko and Ayaka, who had argued over which one of them would teach him, especially at the beginning, had struck a compromise, deciding that "for now, our priority is Kyousuke's education." They were cooperating to coach him.

But the real surprise was Renko's scholarly ability.

Unlike Ayaka, who was checking the books as she taught, Renko sat listening to music. She had drawn terrible portraits of each of them in her neglected notebook. And yet, whenever Kyousuke's pencil would come to a stop on the problem sheet, she would instantly clear up any confusion—"Ah, see, this is…"—and explain the points perfectly.

Even Ayaka was dumbfounded at her intelligence. "I thought, without a doubt, you were feebleminded… It's a fine line between idiot and genius, I suppose." It wasn't clear if she was praising Renko or putting her down.

Renko had said, "It's because my intelligence quotient is five hundred thirty thousand!" but there was no telling with her.

Wearing her headband, eyes full of determination, Maina groaned. "Oh dear! five hundred thirty thousand is too amazing… I can't beat that! Oh no…" She stared down at her workbook covered in Xs, stricken with hopelessness.

Kyousuke understood her feelings all too well. Watching Renko—who really seemed to be a genuine genius—made him feel like his own desperate efforts were doomed to awkward inadequacy. Ayaka was likely the only one among them who could keep up with Renko, though there was one other who showed unblinking valor despite knowing Renko's scholarly ability.

"…I'm sleepy." With an air of unconcern, Eiri rubbed her eyes. Finished with her nails, she stifled a yawn, and stared out the window. Eiri had barely started on her workbook, which sat buried under various manicure tools.

Ayaka finished checking Kyousuke's answers. "Aren't you studying, Miss Washboard?" she asked in apparent surprise.

"…No need."

Renko looked interested. "Oh?" She stood up from her seat. "Perhaps Eiri is smart, too. What's your IQ?"

"…I don't know. I've never been tested."

"Oh, is that so? By the way, mine is five hundred thirty thousand."

"Yeah, yeah…" Eiri waved her hand, as if to wave off the absurdity.

Maina's eyes opened into perfect circles. "A-amazing… She's not even fazed by hearing that number!" Everyone else understood that it was a joke, and no one else was surprised.

"Hmm? So Miss Washboard is also the genius type, huh…? Well, I won't be bested."

"…It doesn't matter. I don't feel like competing anyway." Eiri seemed completely unconcerned with Ayaka's attempts to spark a rivalry. She shook her bare feet, drying her nails.

"Grrrrrr…" Ayaka growled at Eiri, whose calm demeanor remained undisturbed. "What the hell? Are you trying to say that I'm not worthy competition?!"

"Now, now. Eiri is probably a tough opponent, Ayaka! All the nutrition that was supposed to go to her boobs was rerouted to her brain, you see. I estimate her IQ at—one hundred twenty million points!"

At hearing Renko's words, Maina fell out of her chair. "Eeeeeehhh?! One-one h-h-hundred twenty million?!"

Eiri frowned. "…Huh? You're annoying. If you have time to chat, study harder."

"…You really shouldn't be talking, Eiri…"

"Yeah! Geez!" Ayaka waved Eiri off.

"…Tch. I'm good." Eiri brushed her hair aside. "There's no need for me to study. It's a waste of time—"

"Let me see!" Renko grabbed her workbook. "How's your progress?"

Instantly, Eiri's face changed color. "Just a…!!"

She reached out in a panic to try to take the workbook back, but Renko nimbly avoided her grasp. She swiped the workbook out from under the manicure tools, and dashed away from Eiri's seat.

"……A-amazing." Flipping through Eiri's math workbook, Renko let out an astonished murmur. Then she shouted in excitement.

"This is incredible, they're all *wrong*!"

"Huh?"

…*Her answers aren't right… They're all wrong?*

Not paying any mind to Kyousuke and the others, who were visibly taken aback, Renko continued. "There aren't simple arithmetic mistakes; your whole approach to solving the problems is weird! Wow… even these basic problems totally crushed you, huh? That's like…the opposite of amazing! Don't you pay attention in class?"

"Eiri…"

"Eiri…"

"Miss Washboard…"

"_____"

Everyone's gazes fell upon Eiri, who stared out the window.

After a second, she crossed her legs and put one knee up against the desk. "Wh-whatever… This stuff doesn't have anything to do with murder! And it's no use in my daily life! Things like this don't matter to me. What good are equations?" She brushed off their words dismissively.

She spoke confidently, but ultimately she was just being defiant.

"Eiri!" Renko shook her by the shoulders. "You can't escape from reality! Keep this up and you're headed for supplementary lessons!!

And you'll probably fail the supplementary exams, too!! A parole date with Kyousuke is a dream within a dream—"

"Shut up!" Shaking off Renko's arms, Eiri glared at her gas mask. Despite the hard expression in her eyes, large tears welled up in the corners. "I told you, it's no use... I-I don't understand any of it! But I don't want people to think I'm an idiot, and it would be annoying to ask you all to teach me, and there's less than a week left... Even if I score less than half of the average, I think I'll be able to manage somehow, so—" Eiri bit her lip and hung her head.

"Eiri..." Renko whispered, sympathetic. "You don't have boobs or smarts... Just where did your nutrition go?"

"Can't even understand first-year middle school material... Miss Washboard, you are too stupid."

"Eiri...it's not that you didn't want to aim for release on parole, it's that you couldn't."

"Stop it, you guys! She has, well...all kinds of reasons."

Like her family situation. Born and raised in a family of assassins, if Eiri had been given any time to study, she'd surely spent it polishing her killing techniques. Like Kyousuke, who had no time for studying in between fighting and bodybuilding—probably.

"Wh-what the hell... All of you, stop looking at me like that! Math's my weakest subject, so other subjects will be better, or rather, what I mean, ummm..."

"That's enough."

"...Huh?"

Renko spoke in a sorrowful voice, and placed a hand on Eiri's shoulder. "You don't have to put on a brave face anymore, Eiri. I'll teach you. I'll melt away all of your doubts, and ease all of your anxiety. So cheer up, okay? Study for the tests with me."

"Renko..." Her eyes wide, Eiri turned away.

When she spoke, it was with apparent difficulty and a small nod. "I'd...appreciate that."

X   X   X

Noon chimes resounded through the Saturday classroom, empty of its usual occupants due to the off day. Kyousuke finished scribbling in his English vocabulary notebook, put his pencil down, and sighed. Stretching stiff muscles, he checked to see how everyone else was doing.

Renko was fervently instructing Eiri at her desk, now connected to the others. Standing with a textbook grasped in both hands, Eiri read English sentences aloud.

"The death of one is a tragedy."

"No, no, your voice is too quiet. Again!"

"The death of one is a tragedy!"

"Not even close, your feelings are not coming through at all!"

"The death of one is a tragedy!!"

"That's it! 'The death of one is a tragedy'! However—"

"The death of a million is just a statistic!!!"

"Finally, you got it! You memorized the English sentence!"

"Yay, good job! Congratulations!"

Though only an hour had passed, Eiri's studies were progressing well. Maina was also paying attention to Renko's instruction, so Ayaka had Kyousuke all to herself.

"...Tee-hee. It's a good thing that Miss Washboard is an idiot." Gloating, Ayaka moved closer to her brother.

But then her stomach growled, causing her to shriek and dart away, her face turning red. "Eee?! Uh...c-could you pretend like you didn't hear that just now?"

"Don't push yourself, dummy! This is a good stopping place anyway, so why don't we take a break here?"

"...Oooh..." Ayaka hung her head and held her stomach, looking ashamed.

We've lived together our whole lives, but she's embarrassed by a rumbling stomach? Kyousuke smiled and stood up. "Hey, what are you all doing about lunch? I'm going to the school store now."

"Hm?" Renko looked up at the wall clock. "...Aha, it's lunchtime already!"

"Yeah. You all seem busy, so I'll go buy food. What do you want me to get you?" Technically there was *yakisoba* bread available, but since only one load was delivered each day, it usually sold out quickly. There was no way he would make it in time to get some.

"No food for me. I've got my usual jelly packs, but you can get me something to drink!"

"…I'll have rice balls. And tea to drink."

"I'll have, ummm…bread and strawberry milk!" Maina chirped.

"Aha! There we go! Strawberry milk, typical Crafty Cat." Ayaka's reaction was laced with sarcasm.

Maina sank, uncomfortable. "N-not that typical…"

"Got it. Well, we're off on a little errand."

"We probably won't come back the same as we are now, though. Don't take it the wrong way!"

After checking everyone's orders, Kyousuke and Ayaka left the classroom. They walked side by side down the deserted hallway, headed for the school store on the first floor.

"—Oh, Mr. Kamiya!"

As they were descending the stairs, they met a familiar student. She was six feet tall and three feet wide. Her massive frame filled their entire field of vision like a brick wall.

Ayaka let out a scream—"Wah?!"—and jumped into Kyousuke's arms.

From the two eyeholes in the flour sack covering her head, a pair of round, gentle eyes looked down at Ayaka. "This lovely girl is your transfer student sister, is she?"

"B-big brother…who is this person?" Still clinging to Kyousuke's arms, Ayaka looked up at the strange female student. "Or should I ask…what?"

She was clearly frightened.

"Oh, this is Bob. She's in the same Class B as Renko. She may look scary, but she's a good person on the inside, so don't worry. —And this is my little sister, Ayaka."

"Yes. This is our first time meeting, isn't it? How do you do, Ayaka dear?!"

"…P-pleased to meet you…" Ayaka timidly accepted the friendly, outstretched hand.

"Oh-ho-ho!" Bob laughed as they shook hands.

"…Kyousuke's…sister."

Another girl suddenly peeked her face out from behind Bob. She was petite, with long hair, and her blood-red eyes were fixed on Ayaka.

Saliva dripped from the corners of her partly open mouth. "She's not very meaty...but she looks delicious...*gulp*." Baring her well-developed canines, the girl licked her lips.

Ayaka screamed again—"Wah?!"—and hid behind Kyousuke anew.

"Ah...come on! What kind of an introduction is that, Chihiro? How vulgar!" In a panic, Bob picked up her tiny classmate—Chihiro Andou. Wiping away her drool with a handkerchief, Bob quickly apologized. "I'm sorry, Ayaka dear. Chihiro...well, she is extremely fond of human flesh."

"Eh?! H-human...flesh?"

"...Yeah. It's fatty and delicious! Cheek meat, thigh meat...*slurp!*"

"B-big brother...this girl is a little scary."

Ayaka trembled as Chihiro hungrily looked her over. She seemed likely to attack at any moment, were she not restrained by Bob.

Chihiro's blood-red eyes sparkled as Bob rummaged through her handbag. "My goodness! You're really hungry, aren't you? I've got something for you, so be patient!" From her bag she pulled none other than the famed *yakisoba* bread. Beholding this rare article, the seldom-eaten food of legends, Chihiro's eyes sparkled.

"*Chomp.*"

"Ah, owwwwwwwww!!"

Ignoring the bread, she bit down on Bob's fingers. Sinking her fangs into the thick skin, she began to chew. "...*Nom, nom, nom.*"

"Really now," Bob sighed, and picked up the discarded loaf of bread. "...Well, whatever. Anyway, are you studying for the exams, too, Kyousuke?"

"Y-yeah..." Kyousuke nodded as Chihiro continued to gnaw on Bob's fingers. "In one of the open classrooms upstairs, with Renko and the others. Right now we're on our way to buy lunch."

"My goodness, is that so? In that case, sorry for keeping you so long! Chihiro and I are studying in the Class B room, if you feel like coming over."

"Sure, I'll let Renko and the others know. Oh...is Michirou there, too?"

Michirou Suzuki. Otherwise known as Kuuga Makyouin. Something was strange about his left arm; "Azrael," as it was called, could be quite noisy. He did not seem like the ideal study partner.

"I wonder..." Bob tilted her head. "I don't know. Michirou is quite the lone wolf."

"R-really..." It sounded like they had only stuck together during the camping trip because they'd been assigned to the same squad.

"...A friend of yours?" Ayaka asked.

"Friends...? No, I wouldn't say so..."

"My goodness!" Bob laughed sarcastically. "Michirou really is pitiful..." She scooped Chihiro back up. "Well, we're going to head on back now! Study hard! Bye-bye, Ayaka dear. When you have some free time, let's have a nice leisurely tea together, shall we? Oh-ho-ho!"

"Yeah, see you later. You guys work hard, too."

"Good-bye. Unfortunately, I don't think we'll get the chance to have tea, though."

Bob waved a hand at Kyousuke and Ayaka as she set off up the stairs. As they left, Chihiro yelled, "Bye-bye!" and her bloodstained canine teeth sparkled.

Before long, the two figures had disappeared.

"*Haaaaaaahhh*..." As if she was wringing all the air out of her lungs, Ayaka heaved a long sigh. Then she marched around Kyousuke, whirling to glare at him with upturned eyes.

"Big brother, tell me...why do you have only female friends?"

Her piercing eyes seemed to peer right through him.

Kyousuke was overwhelmed by the sudden intensity of his little sister's stare. "Eh? Only girls, that's..."

"They're all girls! Don't you have any guy friends?"

"Of course I do!!"

"For example?"

"F-for example—"

Mohawk, Shinji, Usami, Oonogi... Kyousuke systematically called to mind every male student he knew, and ended up with—

"...Michirou."

"The person who you just said—just a moment ago—is definitely not your friend?"

"Huh?! Th-that's right..." Kyousuke groaned, amazed by her powers of observation.

The look in Ayaka's eyes was growing increasingly hostile, and deep wrinkles were scored into her brow. "Hey, big brother…why is it that you only have female friends?"

Ayaka pressed her face close to his. Her dark eyes seemed like they would devour his shuddering reflection.

"That's just how it happened! I mean, you could say that they all came to me…"

"They all came to you? Why, you really are popular, big brother!" Ayaka grinned as she repeated Kyousuke's words. Unchanging, her eyes did not smile in the slightest.

"H-hey…come on, I'm pretending like I killed twelve people, right? That makes me the top murderer in our class. If this was a normal school, I would be an outcast, but…"

Kyousuke, who had earned nicknames like "Anthrax" and "Metallica," had always scared his female classmates whenever he made eye contact with them, always made them cry whenever he tried to talk to them, was always handed money when he asked for an e-mail address, and had always received terrified apologies following his romantic confessions. However, at this strange school, everything was different. *It was the opposite.*

"Every last student is more fascinated than afraid of the 'Warehouse Butcher.' And since the girls all try to get close to me, the boys are all jealous…"

"So you've made them all your enemies, is that what you're saying?"

"Yeah, that's about right."

"Hmmm…" Ayaka looked away from Kyousuke, eyes downcast. After a moment, she slowly lifted her face and gave her brother a hard look.

"—Are you happy?"

"……Eh?" He looked confused by a question that he did not understand.

Grasping Kyousuke's chest tightly, Ayaka asked him pleadingly, "Does being so popular make you happy? Girls have always avoided you, but now that you're surrounded by them…are you happy? Somehow they're all ridiculously beautiful, too, so of course—"

"Well, maybe."

"......Eh?"

"I mean, it doesn't exactly feel bad to be popular, but...they're all murderers! Most of them are attracted to a crime I didn't even commit! To be honest, it's kind of annoying..."

"Annoying?! It's annoying, big brother?"

Kyousuke smiled wryly at his sister, whose eyes were round and wide, as he recalled the many strange attempts to win his affection. "Of course it is! I'm a normal guy... Naturally I'm not into all that hard-core stuff.

"And no matter how popular I am," he grumbled wearily, "if I died it wouldn't matter anyway." The numerous attempts on his life were nothing to scoff at. Given the chance, he would have changed places with someone else in an instant.

Moved by Kyousuke's suffering, Ayaka winced. "I see..." However, her smile immediately returned. "Of course! You really don't want attention from girls like that... It's annoying, isn't it? Of course! You had me worried, big brother! I was certain you'd become a womanizing playboy. Tee-hee!"

She let go of Kyousuke and started to walk ahead with a nimble gait. The gloomy atmosphere that had surrounded them had vanished and was replaced by a decidedly cheerful air.

Though surprised by the sudden change, Kyousuke readily followed after. "I wish I could become a womanizing playboy," he complained as they walked together. "Then I'd have nothing to worry about."

"Tee-hee! But you've never had a girlfriend, not in your whole life!"

"Shush! The same goes for you..."

"Right, but I've got you, big brother, so I don't need a boyfriend!"

"O-oh..."

"What are you embarrassed about, big brother? Don't tell me you want to make me your girlfriend—"

"No way! You're my sister, not my sweetheart! That relationship will never change."

"Ah-ha-ha, that's right! It definitely, definitely won't ever change, will it?"

"Yeah. No matter what. That's what 'family' means, right?"

"Yep! Until death do us part."

Talking together, they walked down the hallway hand in hand.

"...Yeah. I won't let anything happen to you, even if it costs me my life," he whispered.

Kyousuke squeezed her warm hand softly, which seemed delicate enough to shatter under the slightest pressure. Surrounded by deviants and murders on all sides, Kyousuke wanted desperately to protect that small hand.

You Call That a Knife?

HATE BREED

QUESTION THREE

Q: What is your target rank on the final exams?
I'm going to try hard not to fail!
Also, if possible, I want to score in the top three!

Q: What are your strongest and weakest subjects?
My strongest subject is ethics, and my weakest is home economics.
Cooking is especially...oh dear...

Q: If you are granted parole, what do you want to do?
I would try not to be a nuisance to the rest of the world.
Also, um...visit a grave.

Q: Tell us about your enthusiasm for the tests!
I'w do by bestest!
Ah, I messed it up...
I hope I don't mess up in the answer column. Goodness gracious...

"Can anyone solve this problem?"

The five of them had continued their study party into the night on Saturday, and on Sunday, Kyousuke and Ayaka had studied together alone. Now it was Monday, and their first-period class was mathematics.

Striking the blackboard with an iron pipe stained bright red, Kurumiya looked around at the students. Beneath her feet, a male student with smashed glasses twitched and bled. Kurumiya had forced him to paint a large red X over every mistake on the chalkboard—with his own blood. This gruesome fate befell anyone who gave a wrong answer.

Kurumiya, veins pulsing at her temples, tapped the blackboard again with the pipe. "C'mon! Nobody? —Hah!" She swung downward, crushing the lectern and sending white printouts fluttering through the air.

Kurumiya was in an extremely bad mood thanks to a certain student's shenanigans. On Saturday, that student had stolen Kurumiya's custom motorcycle, driven it around campus, caused an accident, and totaled the bike.

Then on Sunday, just as that student had been about to set off a fireworks festival via grenade launcher, Kurumiya had stuffed him into a cannon and launched him instead. He had become a star in the night sky—or so they thought, until he reappeared Monday morning in the main hall, enthusiastically breakdancing with Kurumiya's underwear on his head.

Kurumiya's anger had reached new heights that morning. The last outburst had seen a third student fall victim to the iron pipe. The rest of the class huddled quietly, afraid to raise a hand. Nobody wanted to volunteer an answer, no matter how confident they might be.

"Yes! I know!"

Ayaka, sitting to Kyousuke's right, spoke up in a cheerful voice. She stretched her hand straight up in the air, wearing an expression full of confidence.

"Good. Little Miss Kamiya, get your butt to the front."

"Yes, ma'am!"

Ayaka stood before the blackboard, writing gracefully, as the medical team carried the discarded male student out on a stretcher. Watching his little sister's gallant figure, Kyousuke thought he could feel his life grow shorter by the moment.

"—That's correct." Drawing a circle around the answer in red, Kurumiya tousled Ayaka's hair. Her furious facial expression had disintegrated in an instant and was replaced by a bright smile. The cheerful grin perfectly suited her cherubic, childlike face.

"......?!"

The class erupted into noise. They had never seen Kurumiya wear such a kind expression. Beside her, Ayaka seemed embarrassed. The two of them together looked like they could be sisters, or close friends.

"Volunteering under pressure, showing no fear, and writing the correct answer—splendid!" Kurumiya sounded like an altogether different person as she showered Ayaka with praise. "Your courage is remarkable! Even though you just transferred, your answer is perfect. Bravo!"

"Thank you very much, Miss Kurumiya!"

"Hmm... Little Miss Kamiya is an excellent student. Her brother must be so proud."

"......"

To see Kurumiya openly praise a student was truly unprecedented, and the class stared, dumbfounded as their demonic instructor showed kindness for the first time. Her sweet expression and frank words did not seem to belong to the Kurumiya they knew.

On the other hand, Ayaka, who had just transferred in at the end of the past week, simply looked delighted. With no misgivings at all about Kurumiya's behavior, she returned triumphantly to her seat.

"You piggies should all follow your classmate's example! The end-of-term exams are next week, after all. Failure to solve problems of this level is inexcusable! I want to see you get the next one right—understand?!"

"Yes, ma'am!"

"Good answer. Now keep it up!"

"Yes, ma'am!"

"All right. Now, if I see even one of you with your hand down, it'll be a genocide!" Kurumiya's canines glittered as she began to explain the math problem. Her terrible mood seemed to have softened, at least a little, and the rest of the class unfolded under a peaceful air of brutal oppression, during which she had thankfully few occasions to wield absurd violence.

I thought Kurumiya would be the biggest threat to Ayaka, but...

"Next is question four, part two. Miss Kamiya, your answer!"

"Yes, ma'am! $x = 7$."

"Correct. You really are good. I expect you to do this well on the exams, too!"

"Eee-hee-hee...I'll do my best, Miss Kurumiya!"

Rather than picking on Ayaka, Kurumiya praised her, and instead of lashing out at her, she patted her gently on the head. Kyousuke was completely baffled.

After flattering Ayaka, Kurumiya looked pointedly at him. "On the other hand, the regular Kamiya...good grief! Who would imagine that two siblings could be this different? Aren't you embarrassed? You should try to learn from your sister's example, you dumb bunny."

"...S-sorry." Kyousuke was used to being compared to his little sister, and it was true that she was an excellent student. He took pride in her as her older brother, but—

"Tee-hee!" Ayaka laughed. "Don't worry about it, big brother!"

She did not seem at all upset by Kyousuke's abuse. From the way she looked, it was almost like she had taken to idolizing Kurumiya...

Kyousuke's heart was heavy indeed.

X   X   X

"Yes, I know you think that Kurumiya is a good teacher, but..."

First period had ended, and they were on a break. Ayaka was scowling as Kyousuke tried to warn her not to trust their instructor.

Kyousuke shook his head. "Kurumiya is the kind of person who turns violent at the drop of a hat. It doesn't even matter if you're a girl! She might be smiling now, but deep down you have no idea what she's thinking. And don't forget, I've suffered quite a lot, too, you know. Seriously, be careful around the teachers here."

Ayaka listened to her brother's serious advice, her expression unchanging. Looking around the graffiti-covered, crumbling classroom, her eyebrows knit suspiciously.

"Watch out for the teachers, you say...? Shouldn't it be just the opposite? This is a school for reforming murderers, right? So shouldn't I be worried about the students, rather than the teachers? It's not like the students are innocent victims, are they...?

"And besides, you're supposed to have killed twelve people, big brother. Are you surprised they're keeping a close eye on you?"

"...Um." Kyousuke couldn't argue with Ayaka's words. He'd actually thought the same things himself, before he'd learned of the academy's true nature. This school wasn't interested in reforming murderers. It was a training ground for professional killers. Kurumiya and the other teachers were killers themselves, far more dangerous than the murderers they oversaw. Kyousuke wavered, wondering if he ought to tell Ayaka the truth, but—

He didn't want any other students overhearing them. He would have to find another opportunity. Murder training didn't start until the second year, and the truth was kept hidden from the underclassmen. "Anyway, I'll tell you why Kurumiya is dangerous later. First, let's go somewhere else."

"Uh, okay... I don't really understand, but okay." Ayaka followed reluctantly as Kyousuke rose from his seat. Second and third periods included hands-on instruction, so they had to change classrooms.

"Okay. Well, let's get going."

Home economics class was held on the first floor, on the west side of the building, quite far from Kyousuke's first-year Class A classroom, which was in the middle of the second floor.

"...*Yawn*..."

"Oh dear..."

Eiri and Maina joined them as they left the classroom. Together, they descended the east stairs and headed down the first-floor hallway toward the home economics classroom.

Their route was somewhat indirect, and none of their classmates were around. It was practically deserted.

"This school has cooking classes just like a regular school, huh?!" Ayaka's voice was lively in the silence. As she walked down the long hallway, she swung the cloth bag containing her apron and bandanna. Her gait was even lighter than usual. "I'm so happy...hee-hee-hee! After sooo long, you can finally eat my home cooking again! I'm going to make something really special, big brother!"

"Ayaka's home cooking, huh...?" Thinking about it, Kyousuke realized he hadn't eaten his sister's cooking in over half a year. He had halfway given up on ever tasting it again. Tears welled up in Kyousuke's eyes as he felt overcome by the surge of emotions. "Ah, I'm seriously insanely looking forward to this. I'm drooling just from imagining it..."

"The food here is pretty disgusting, isn't it?"

"For sure. I'm getting sick just thinking about it—"

"...Hmm? Can you cook?" Eiri asked, speaking up from her position tailing the rest of the group. She suddenly seemed very interested in the conversation.

Ayaka turned around and nodded. "Of course! Cooking and cleaning are the measure of a good wife, after all. I'm sure you're really good at that sort of thing, right, Miss Akabonehead?"

"Akabonehead?"

It seemed that Eiri's nickname had changed from "Miss Washboard." Eiri did not look bothered. "...I can do better than Maina."

"Ehh?!" Maina exclaimed, an unsuspecting victim of a careless verbal attack.

Ayaka laughed. "Tee-hee! Crafty Cat, you must really stink, huh? Mixing up sugar and salt, that kind of stuff."

"......"

"Huh, did I hit the bull's-eye?" Ayaka looked at Kyousuke and the others, who stayed silent, with an incredulous expression.

As a matter of fact, the problems with Maina's cooking went far beyond mixing up sugar and salt. It was impossible to explain what Maina did to make her food turn out the way it did. She was probably the last person on earth who should have been allowed to cook.

"I mean... Big brother, could it possibly be that you've eaten food made by Miss Akabonehead and Crafty Cat?" Ayaka demanded. "Well...have you?!"

Her voice grew low, and there was a dangerous expression in her upturned eyes.

Kyousuke shuddered as he recalled the Outdoor Cooking disaster. He didn't really understand why Ayaka was angry but immediately decided to deny everything. "No, I haven't. Although...I have seen them cook before."

Luckily—if it could be called that—Kyousuke had missed his chance to eat at the Outdoor Cooking event, and since they had been divided into cooking teams according to seat numbers, would probably never have another chance to eat their cooking. Although, to be honest, he wouldn't have volunteered to eat anything either of them had prepared anyway.

"...That's right." Eiri averted her gaze.

"He hasn't!" Maina agreed without a moment's delay, waving her hands in distress. "I would never ask him to eat my cooking...it's..." She hung her head low.

Ayaka tilted her head at the unexpected response. "Huh? You understand me perfectly well, don't you, Crafty Cat? That's riiight. If you made my big brother eat your terrible cooking, and it made him sick... that would be just awful!"

Maina laughed self-consciously. "Oh my...he'd be lucky if he only got sick!"

Ayaka seemed to think that Maina was joking, and she adopted an exaggerated tone. "Yes, yes! If it was just a matter of mixing up sugar and salt, that would be fine...but mixing up sugar and arsenic, or salt and strychnine, or pepper and potassium cyanide is no joking matter, is it? Killer cooking—that would be crazy!"

"Ah, ah-ha-ha...th-that's right!" Maina's smile twitched. Ayaka's joke had missed the mark, but not by much.

"...Ah!" Ayaka started, as if she had suddenly realized something significant. "You're also a murderer, Crafty Cat, so something like that wouldn't be too out of place for someone like you, would it? Like, if you were the 'Killer Cook' who pretended to prepare loving, home-cooked meals, only to serve up *deadly home-cooked meals!* Cunniiing! Tee-hee! You're totally capable of something like that!"

"...?! Uh oh—!" Eiri quickly tried to restrain Maina, but—

"Whoooooooaaaaaa?!"

Maina, shaken by Ayaka's words, tripped over her own feet. The fall was magnificent.

"Waaaaaaaaahhhhhh?!" Just as he had begun to turn and look back, Kyousuke, caught in Maina's path, was thrown off his feet.

He landed on his back with a heavy grunt.

"Aieeeee?!"

Maina was straddling Kyousuke.

"Big brother?!"

"...Are you guys okay?"

Ayaka and Eiri stared down at the two of them in a heap, looking concerned. Maina had her face buried in Kyousuke's chest, as if he were holding her in his arms.

"Uhh...yeah, I think so." Despite aching from his hip to his shoulder on his left side, Kyousuke didn't seem to be injured. He pushed himself up off the floor. "Hey, are you all right, Maina? Did you get hurt in the fall...?"

"Ah...I'm, I'm fine! Thanks to you, Kyousuke—"

"Then why are you clinging to hiiiiiiiiiiiiiiiiiiiiiiiiimmmmmmmm mmmmmmm?!"

"Eeek?!"

As Maina raised her face to look, Ayaka shoved her away. She tumbled over, falling hard on the hallway floor.

Ayaka stared down at her. "What were you doing clinging to him, using the confusion as cover, Crafty Cat... That fall just now, that was on purpose, wasn't it?! Seriously, stop doing things like that!"

"Ehh?! S-sorry...but, umm, it wasn't on purpose..."

"It was *too* on purpose! Nobody is stupid enough to trip and fall over nothing at all!"

"Hey, Ayaka—!" Kyousuke rushed over to the two of them.

"What is it?" Ayaka demanded. She glared at Maina, who was still flailing around in a panic.

Though still wary of her threatening tone, Kyousuke tried to calm his sister. "Give it a rest! It really was not on purpose."

"No way! She absolutely meant to fall down!" Pointing at Maina, Ayaka puffed out her cheeks. "I saw it myself. Crafty Cat *tripped herself on her own two feet*. That had to have been intentional!"

"Ayaka, you...haven't heard Maina's story yet, have you?"

"...Her story?"

"About the murder Maina committed..."

"I don't know anything about it, and I don't care! Though I did hear that Crafty Cat has killed three people, and Miss Akabonehead has killed six... I don't know how you killed them or anything. Anyway you probably slashed them with a blade, or strangled them or something, right? I haven't heard all the details—"

"Clumsiness and cooking."

"...Eh?"

"Maina killed people with clumsiness and cooking."

"Uh, umm..."

"Let me tell you about it, Ayaka," Maina said.

She stood and explained her story as Ayaka listened with a dumbfounded expression. She described how she was predisposed to kill people with her own clumsiness, and how people had died from food that she had made, and how neither was on purpose, and how Maina herself had no malicious intent, and how until now she had kept it to herself, imagining that anyone she tried to tell would be sure to keep their distance...

Finally Maina finished with "I'm sorry," and hung her head.
"Ah, so that's how it is, huh…?" Ayaka asked with a smile.

"*In that case, never go near my big brother, ever again.*"

"_____"

Maina was speechless.
"I mean, it's far too dangerous, isn't it?!" Ayaka continued, her smile fading. "If you're with him, who knows when he might be killed by that clumsiness… It's easy enough to avoid your cooking, but what if he's in another accident, like the one you just caused? What then? If you can't control it, doesn't that make you even more dangerous? From now on, I want you to stay at least six feet away from my big brother at all times! You understand me, right, Crafty Cat?"

"*I refuse.*"

Maina brushed aside Ayaka's demand.
"……Eh?" Ayaka looked flabbergasted. No doubt she hadn't been expecting an argument.
Maina stared at Ayaka with purposeful eyes. Her frail bearing had completely changed. "I'm sorry, Ayaka. I just can't agree to your request. Maybe if you didn't want me to come close to you…it would be sad, but I would try to stay away. But Kyousuke told me that it would be all right! No matter how clumsy I am, or how awkward, no matter how much trouble I cause, it's all right, he said… He would be with me, he said! So, I'm sorry. I have no intention of leaving Kyousuke's side."

"Wha……" Ayaka's eyes were wide. Her mouth noiselessly opened and closed, and her body shook with silent rage. "Th-this…what… making a self-centered, reckless remark—"

"Sorry, Ayaka. It's like Maina says."

"…Big…brother?" Ayaka, her angry words interrupted, stared at Kyousuke in blank amazement.
Kyousuke looked down, as if to escape Ayaka's gaze, and continued.

"I know about Maina's clumsiness. And I believe that I know very well the harm that Maina's clumsiness can cause. She's incredibly earnest, and tries with all her might, and battles on in the face of difficulty, so...even if it is a little bit dangerous, I still want to be with her."

"Kyousuke..."

"_____"

Ayaka's eyes turned dark.

Kyousuke did not seem to notice the change in his little sister, and continued to try to persuade her. "Besides, it's not like Maina will cause a disaster whenever or wherever. If we're very careful, she can lead a normal life. And besides, I only *almost* died the very first time that Maina even had an accident, so...she's not as dangerous as you say!"

He looked up, searching for his sister's reaction.

"_____"

This time it was Ayaka who was looking down, her expression hidden beneath the shadow cast by her loosely hanging bangs.

"And you don't need to worry about the times when she *is* dangerous. No matter how clumsy Maina gets, I'll be here to protect you, Ayaka! Won't you trust me? And try to get along with her? You and Maina are almost the same age, and I really think you could become good friends."

"_____"

"Uh, Sis?" Kyosuke moved to stretch out a hand toward the absolutely motionless girl.

"......that......to you...?" Ayaka muttered quietly.

"Huh? Sorry, you're too quiet and I can't hear—"

"Is this girl really that important to you?!"

Ayaka howled hysterically, her voice echoing in the still hallway. Glaring at Kyousuke, she pointed at Maina and shut her lips tight, as if there was nothing more to say.

Kyousuke took a deep breath, trying to recover his composure.

"Yes, she is important. Maina is my dear friend."

"......?!"

The moment Kyousuke answered, Ayaka's eyes, which recalled the surface of still, black water, wavered. As if that vibration was rippling outward, her shoulders, then her fists, then her whole body—began to tremble. "I-is that how it is? You put your friends before your own sister... Yes, I understand. I understand perfectly..."

She unclenched her fists, and the strength seemed to drain immediately from her body. Her stiff expression slackened, and a broad smile spread across Ayaka's face.

"If that's how it is, I guess you can just do whatever you like!"

She turned and walked away briskly.

"......Eh?" Kyousuke couldn't do anything but stare at Ayaka's back as she moved farther and farther away. Her steps were quiet, but it was clear that she was raging.

A hand clapped the dumbfounded Kyousuke on the back. "...Don't worry about it." Leaving him with that single phrase, Eiri followed after Ayaka.

Kyousuke continued to stand, unresponsive.

Maina shyly pulled at his hand. "Kyousuke, let's go, too. We'll be late to class."

"Hmm...? O-oh..." Kyousuke finally came to his senses, and started walking as he had been told. His limbs felt like they were not his own. They had no power. The inside of his head was vacant except for the echo of Ayaka's words. He couldn't think of anything else as he shuffled aimlessly forward. And yet—

"I'm sorry, but...thank you."

Maina's voice, halting but full of joy, brought warmth to Kyousuke's chest.

X X X

"Uh, um...Sis?"

"_____"

Ayaka completely ignored Kyousuke's timid words, keeping her gaze fixed on the handle of her knife as she continued smoothly chopping. Her cheeks were puffed up so large that they looked like they might pop.

The chives on her cutting board were being very finely minced indeed.

"Uh, ummm…"

"Ayaka," called another member of their group, "I finished peeling the potatoes!"

The moment he did, Ayaka burst into a wide smile. "Oh, okay! Thank you very much," she replied courteously. "Would you please dip them in water?"

"Yes, ma'am!" The male student bowed and quickly moved to follow her instructions.

Ayaka, who had finished chopping the chives, started on an onion, still smiling brightly.

"Hey, Ayaka!" Kyousuke cheerfully inquired, sensing an opportunity. "Don't you have anything that I could help with?"

"_____"

The smile instantly vanished from Ayaka's face as she continued to cut vegetables, completely ignoring him.

Undaunted, Kyousuke tried again to get through to her. "Hey, hey! I'll do anything, okay? If it's something I can do, I'll do anything!"

"……so……you…?"

Ayaka's hand suddenly stopped.

"Ah, yes?!" Happy to have finally gotten a response, Kyousuke sounded more and more lively. "What'd you say? If it's a request from you, with all my strength—"

"You're just in the way, so get out of here, would you?!"

"……Okay."

Ayaka waved her knife at Kyousuke as he left the kitchen counter in tears.

He came to stand beside the window, where he looked around the classroom, feeling like a shriveled green vegetable.

The students, in their bandannas and aprons, worked together in groups of four, harmoniously practicing cooking.

Kurumiya, wearing a matronly apron, patrolled the space between the kitchen counters, watching the students carefully. On her shoulder she carried an enormous wooden spoon in place of the usual iron pipe.

*　　*　　*

"Keep it up, worms! Do your best, heh-heh-heh! This is your one chance to eat a decent meal!"

Kurumiya laughed and struck a male student, who had been trying to steal her kitchen knife, on the head with the wooden spoon.

Many ingredients had been arranged on a silver table at the front of the classroom. Onions, carrots, potatoes, cabbage, lettuce, bok choy, spinach, tomatoes, bell peppers, pumpkins, shiitake mushrooms, pork, chicken, beef, bacon, eggs…et cetera. Most of it was in poor condition, and some of the food even looked mostly rotten. The students were to select their ingredients, refer to the recipe in their textbooks, and practice cooking together in groups—that was "cooking class," Purgatorium Remedial Academy–style.

Ayaka had taken command in Kyousuke's group, and was working diligently at her meal.

It had been thirty minutes since the start of second period. Every group had made different amounts of progress, and there were even some groups that still hadn't started cooking. For example—

"Please! I'm really begging you, Miss Eiri. We'll do anything to try your home cooking. Look, like this! Like this, no seriously!"

"Hee-hee-hee…peeping at panties…peeping at panties while prostrating plainly…Hee-hee—gyah?!"

Two male students groveled on their hands and knees, heads bowed. One wore dreadlocks, and the other had a hunchback.

"…Huh? Are you seriously making a pass at me now? Don't you have any shame? You're garbage, like vegetable scraps." Looking down at Oonogi and stepping on Usami's head, Eiri snorted. "…Hmph."

"Oh dear… E-Eiri…let's leave it there…oh no…" Maina held on to Eiri's hem in a panic.

"Ah?! You bastard, that's clever! I want to be stepped on by Miss Eiri—gah!!"

Eiri blushed, and stomped on Oonogi's face. "Y-you pervert… shut up!"

Oonogi twisted beneath her foot, mouth hanging open. "Gyaaah?! St-sto—ah, don't stop…sto-stop iiiiit!!"

"Hee-hee...panties, panties, before my eyes...hee-hee-hee...!"

"Oh goodness! Give it up already, Eiri! These guys are hard-core perverts! Let's just make them something to eat..."

"Fine, whatever! Let's just do it already!"

"Yahoooooo!" Oonogi and Usami cheered and high-fived.

"...Just die."

Eiri glared at them as she tied her apron.

"Looks like they're having fun...not that I'm jealous, though," Kyousuke muttered.

Maina had been relegated to observing. She was barred from doing any actual cooking.

With mixed feelings, Kyousuke watched Oonogi and Usami skipping around the kitchen counter. Ha! The two of them probably had no idea how bad Eiri's cooking really was—

"Well, then... Now we just simmer it like this, right?" From nearby wafted the rich aroma of soy sauce and mirin. Ayaka stood catching her breath in front of a simmering pot, having somehow already finished her first dish. She was incredibly industrious.

Ayaka handed her ladle to another student, who stood peering into the pot. "Kitou, while you watch it boil, would you please skim the top of the liquid? And Kousaka, please skin these with the vegetable peeler. This is a special occasion, so let's give it our best and make all kinds of things!" She pumped her fist in the air as she gave the two boys their instructions.

"Oh, oh, oh!" Their eyes sparkled as they leaped to their duties.

If he could have, Kyousuke would have changed places with the two in a heartbeat, but before he could speak up, he was met with a cold voice and scornful eyes.

"...I told you to get out of here, didn't I?"

Her kitchen knife landed with a heavy blow, cleanly bisecting the head of a mackerel.

"......I suppose."

Kyousuke slunk away from the kitchen counter, dejected. Ayaka seemed extremely angry that he had taken Maina's side. This was the first time she'd ever lashed out at him so harshly, and he didn't know how to respond. Instead he just gave up, and sat cross-legged in a corner of the classroom.

"Kyousuke, um…a-are you okay?"

When Kyousuke lifted his head, he saw Maina staring down at him, looking concerned. She crouched down beside him. "It's because of me…isn't it? I'm so sorry… Ayaka is really angry—"

"Don't worry about it," Kyousuke interrupted, placing a hand on Maina's head. "You didn't do anything wrong, Maina. This is all Ayaka's fault…I think. No…is it mine? Yeah, this is all my fault. I phrased things badly, and that's why Ayaka is so—"

"Kyousuke, you've done nothing wrong!" Maina insisted firmly, before immediately returning to her usual, frail voice. "Kyousuke, you're not bad…though I don't mean to say that Ayaka is bad, either. I think anyone would get upset when someone important to them was in some kind of danger, so…of course we weren't going to get along right away. I think it will take some time. My accidents can be pretty dangerous, after all. It's not easy for me to accept it myself… I think I understand her feelings."

With her large, flax-colored eyes, Maina gazed intently into Kyousuke's, her voice filled with conviction. "But that's even more reason not to give up! I'll try my hardest to make Ayaka trust me! It was probably too soon before. She needed to accept my clumsiness before I could get her to trust me… I think so, anyway. That's why I'll become good friends with Ayaka first! I will get her to trust me…she'll feel the same way about me that you do, Kyousuke!"

"Maina…" When she put it like that, Kyousuke had to believe her. *You can't just tell someone to trust a person; they have to learn to trust them on their own.* It was sure to be difficult, especially for someone like Maina. "Yeah…yeah, I think you're right. We were probably a little impatient…"

"Yes. I'm also going to apologize later. Let's make peace!"

"…Yeah. Thanks, Maina. I'm feeling a lot better, thanks to you."

Kyousuke smiled warmly and stroked Maina's hair.

The girl smiled bashfully and let it happen.

"_____"

Ayaka stared at the two of them from the kitchen counter. Her knife stopped in the middle of gutting a mackerel, and her eyes clouded over like the fish's.

Kyousuke and Maina did not seem to notice.

Oblivious, they stood close and continued their friendly conversation.

"......That girl."

Ayaka's molars ground audibly. The point of her knife severed the mackerel's spine.

X   X   X

"Ohhh...you made *all* of this, Ayaka?" Kyousuke asked, astonished.

Meat and potato stew, mackerel cooked in miso, fried chicken, rolled omelets, boiled spinach, miso soup...so many dishes crowded for space on the table top, garnished with chives and ginger and shredded daikon piled up beside every plate. And he knew perfectly well that Ayaka's food tasted just as good as it looked.

He swallowed in anticipation, then paused. "Umm... Sis?" Kyousuke asked timidly. "There's no plate for me..."

There was nothing in front of Kyousuke but a cup of tap water. Meanwhile, in front of Ayaka (seated next to him) and the other students (seated across from him), individual plates had been laid out next to bowls of white rice and miso soup.

Kyousuke hadn't even been given a pair of chopsticks.

Ayaka smiled and answered flatly,

"There's no reason there would be."

"......Seriously?"

"Yep. I mean, you didn't help at all, big brother. Those who don't work don't eat."

"B-but when I tried, you said 'get out of here'—"

"Did I?"

"Yeah..."

"I don't remember that."

"......"

Kyousuke glared at her with scornful eyes, but Ayaka was completely unfazed. "In the first place, you're only reaping what you've sown! It wouldn't be so bad if you had just skipped out on work, but then you had to go and get all flirty-flirty with a classmate! I will not share a meal with such a bad person. I sentence you to going without dinner. Please reflect on your mistakes veeeeeery carefully."

"Flirty-flirty? …Weren't those your words?"

Previously, following Ayaka and Maina's earlier confrontation, as soon as it was time for a break from cooking, Kyousuke had approached Ayaka to apologize.

Maina had also come, and bowed in apology, but Ayaka's response had been—

"You're in the way of my cooking. Would you move? Aren't you useless people satisfied with your flirty conversation?! Stay out of my sight!"

"……"

"……"

— Kyousuke and Maina had been faced with no choice but to turn back around and convene another meeting in the corner of the classroom.

They had concluded that, for the time being, it would be best to stay out of the way and wait for Ayaka to calm down.

…And now Kyousuke could not believe that, after waiting a good while before trying to go back, he had still received a starvation sentence.

"…Ah, I'm sorry! The food that we went to so much trouble to make has gotten cold, hasn't it? My idiot older brother was such a bother… Well, anyway, please eat up!" Ayaka clapped her hands cheerfully.

"Hooraaaaaay!" the male students shouted happily. They took up their chopsticks, and after pressing their hands together and saying, "Thank you for the meal!" they tackled each other to get to the meat and potato stew and fried food.

"Bwuh———?!"

From the next table over came the loud sounds of someone spitting. Oonogi and Usami appeared to be choking. Across from them, Maina shrieked and leaped out of the path of the spray. Oonogi and Usami were writhing in horrible agony, feebly gasping for air.

"Wh...what the hell is thiiiiiis?! Tough...it's ridiculously tough... half-cooked, isn't it...and yet, it stinks—is it rotten?! This food is rotteeeeeen!!"

"Hee-hee-hee...sweet and salty, bitter and sour...the flavor is a mess. The food is a mess! It's a catastrophe in my moooooouth. Hee-hee... ohhh!"

"_____"

Eiri, covered in their expelled food, glared wordlessly at both of them. Sitting between the two, on the table across from Eiri, was a single dish piled up on a platter. It was arranged in a tall heap that looked like it would collapse at any moment. Random ingredients had been tossed haphazardly together and thoroughly boiled. The pitiful dish resembled a mountain of mangled corpses.

Eiri had once again caused a tragedy. She pressed a hand to her forehead. "Y-you guys...you said you'd do anything to try my cooking, so what's with those faces? You want to die? You'd be better off dead."

"Oh dear, oh my... Your pretty face is dirty now...oh no..." Maina wiped at Eiri with her pink handkerchief.

Oonogi and Usami, back on their feet, tried to explain their way out of trouble.

"B-but listen...we never thought that you would make such terrible 'food,' Miss Eiri. You're just too unladylike! This is the worst thing I've eaten in my entire life!"

"Hee-hee...don't call it 'food,' it's just ordinary garbage. It's compost...hee-hee-hee..."

"Wha—" Eiri looked stunned, and her face flushed red. "Shut up, both of you! You've really gone too far! I don't care what you say, there's no way it can be that bad! It's not like it has anything weird in it! Don't be ridiculous!!" Furiously, she snatched up her chopsticks and shoveled up a big mouthful.

"_____"

After a moment's hesitation, she swallowed, barely taking time to chew. "Oh, gross—I mean...it's delicious...yeah...that's it..."

Beads of sweat and a stiff smile appeared on her face.

"No, no, no, no!" Oonogi jabbed back. "You're totally forcing it, aren't you? Your face is pale!!"

"...H-huh? No way! I'm telling you guys, it's really grooooo—wing on me!"

"Seriously? Well, you can have the rest—"

Eiri cut this off at the pass. "...Hmm, I'm full."

"You've only eaten one bite!! What a small stomach you must have!!"

"Um, excuse me...I also have a small appetite, so..."

"Hey! Don't think you can just sneak away, clumsy girl."

"Hee-hee-hee...m-my stomach...it feels...I'm going to the bath-room!"

"I won't let you run away, Usami!! One person can't eat this much alone, ya know."

"By the way, if you leave any behind, you'll face serious discipline. You made it, so be sure to clean your plates!"

"Gah?! M-Ms. Kurumiya...but...Akabane was the one who—"

"Eh...? I seem to remember the two of you asking her. Now eat up."

"B-but—"

"Now. Eat. UP."

"......Yes, ma'am."

Under Kurumiya's bloodthirsty gaze, Oonogi and Usami gripped their chopsticks and prepared to dig in. Sweat, tears, and snot flowed from their anguished faces as they approached the "meal"—

"De...deliciooooooouuuuuussssss!"

In contrast to Oonogi and Usami's living hell, the two male students tasting Ayaka's food shouted in excitement as they sampled the many dishes that she had prepared.

"This meat and potato stew is so full of flavor...the meat and veggies soaked in broth really melt in your mouth! Forget home cooking, this is fine dining! I-I'm touched..."

"Wow!! The outside is crisp...the inside is juicy...every bite explodes with flavor! Even the batter on this fried chicken is a masterpiece!"

Ayaka puffed up her chest as she listened to their rave reviews. "Ahem. It's because I started the meat and potato stew with dashi stock, and because I fried the chicken just before dishing it up! If you put my special sauce on it instead of lemon juice, it'll transform into Chinese-style fried chicken."

"Whoooaaa, amaaazing! Ayaka's amaaazing!"

"I think I love you, Ayaka, more than anyone else! Marry me, pleeeaaase!"

"…Huh? Who's going to let you have Ayaka? I'll kill you!"

"Yes, yes…" Ayaka brushed Kyousuke aside. He had kicked over his chair as he stood up. "I wonder if we should even let my big brother have water…? Oh, Mister Kitou! Do you need a second helping of rice? You eat plenty, too, Mister Kousaka!"

"Okaaaaaaaaayyy!"

They pumped their fists in the air.

Kyousuke, who had received a "starvation sentence," could do nothing but stare, looking on enviously as they ate. His stomach growled as if in lamentation. He had been looking forward to this since before class had started. This abuse was just too much.

"Wha—?! Big brother, what are you crying for?"

"Waaah…because you're…y-you're…*hic*…!"

Kyousuke could not hold back. He cried a great deal. Ayaka drew away, startled, and even Kitou and Kousaka stopped eating. His classmates turned to stare, and he could hear their mutters circulate around the room.

"Wha…look! That Kamiya guy is seriously crying!! Tears come even to the eyes of murderers, huh…"

"What's that, a brother-sister fight? But it looks like Kyousuke's losing big time!"

"Other people's misery makes the best side dish. It's really improving the flavor of my meal! It's my favorite spice. Eee-hee-hee!"

"Gya-ha-ha! What a major dork. That guy's got a seriously messed-up sister complex. Eeewww…"

"Oh dear…Kyou-Kyousuke…"

"…Let's leave him here and go. The school store is gonna be crowded soon."

Glancing sidelong at the sobbing Kyousuke, Eiri and Maina quickly left the classroom.

"Big brother…" Ayaka's voice was full of shock and pity. But she quickly shook her head. "No, no! Big brother is going without, that's final! I have to teach you a lesson about what you did... I can't spoil you, no way! I'm not going to forgive you, you know!!"

"Waaah...Ayakaaa..."

"I-I won't give you any, even if you make those Chihuahua eyes!" As if to escape Kyousuke's pleading gaze, Ayaka turned to face away from her brother. She continued her meal with a resolute demeanor. No matter what Kyousuke said, she absolutely would not accede—her intentions were crystal clear.

Kyousuke's depression seemed to cast a gloomy air over the table. Even Kitou and Kousaka grew quiet. The meal they had worked so hard to prepare was ruined.

This is just too much... Sensing that his presence was nothing but a nuisance, Kyousuke quietly stood up from his seat. He would have to head to the cafeteria or school store if he wanted to find lunch.

"......Hmph."

Ayaka huffed but didn't try to stop him.

"Yoo-hoo, everyone! I came to see you! Did you make some tasty food?"

Suddenly, a friendly voice rang out from the doorway, where a female student wearing a black gas mask was energetically waving.

X   X   X

"Renko..."

"*Kksshh.* What happened, Kyousuke? You're making a face like you might die any minute now. Did you eat something bad— waaaaaaaaaaaahhh!!" As she approached Kyousuke's table, Renko reared back in surprise. "Wh-wwwwh-what the hell is this wonderful cuisine?! Who on earth—?"

"I did," Ayaka answered bluntly, and sipped her miso soup.

"What did you saaay?!" Renko was even more taken aback. "*You* made everything on this table all by yourself, Ayaka?!"

"Yep. I did have help from Kitou and Kousaka, though."

"Kitou and Kousaka... Who are they?"

"It's us, GMK!"

The two threw down their chopsticks and stood up simultaneously. Standing so straight they were almost bent backward, they were faintly flushed in the cheeks.

Renko clapped her hands in recognition. "Oh! Aren't you the boys who helped us start the fire during the Outdoor Cookout?"

"…Eh? Ah…y-yes!" Kitou and Kousaka seemed very happy to be recognized by their idol GMK—by Renko, and after exchanging glances, they bowed back at her vigorously.

"…GMK?" Ayaka knit her brows.

"That's the stage name I use with Fuckin' Park. I'm 'Gas Mask'—GMK."

"Oh? So you are a comedian after all?"

Though she was actually a musical artist, Renko nodded anyway. "Yeah. Sometime I'll do a live show just for you, Ayaka! I don't play around, I take my shows very seriously…*kksshh*. Anyway, enough of that—"

Her viewports shining, Renko returned her gaze to the table, surveying the impressive spread. "This is really amazing…and everything looks so delicious, doesn't it! I thought it might be from some three-star restaurant. Turning those garbage ingredients into something like this… Are you a genius, Ayaka? It's just like magic! Your feminine prowess is just too muuuuuuuuuch!"

"…Mmm." Ayaka's disinterested facade crumbled under Renko's praise. A broad smile spread across her face—or started to, before she tightened her mouth into a frown, and put on a sullen expression. "It-it's not that big of a deal. Please stop with the obvious flattery."

"It's not flattery! Oh, I wish I could take off this mask right now just to taste your cooking… Maybe I could have some miso soup? Look, I'll use this straw tube and suck it up."

"No way. I refuse."

"It's okay. Come ooooon! I'm fine with just broth from the meat and potato stew, or the fried chicken sauce, or the grated daikon on the rolled omelets! I want to taste your food, Ayaka baaaby!"

"Just a…aah, no, get off me!" Ayaka glared at the gas mask as she tried to shake off Renko's embrace.

Placing an index finger against the exhaust port, Renko mumbled, "…Stingy."

"I'm fine with being stingy. I didn't make this food for you, anyway."

"Is that so? And who did you make it for, I wonder?"

"Umm…th-that's…" Ayaka faltered. Her eyes briefly wandered through space. "For Mr. Kitou and Mr. Kousaka—"

"Yeah, sure. It was for Kyousuke, wasn't it?"

"……?!" Ayaka's body shook with a start.

Renko laughed. "*Kksshh!* You wouldn't have gone to all this trouble otherwise, would you? I knew that you loved Kyousuke, but when I saw this spread, I really, truly believed it. Of course the number of dishes shows it, but each one also took an awful lot of time and effort. It's obvious how much you care about whoever you made this for."

"_____"

Ayaka bit her lip and did not answer.

As if she had only just noticed a crucial detail, Renko tilted her head curiously. "And yet…huh? The important party—Kyousuke—hasn't eaten yet, has he! How cruel, Kyousuke!! She went to all the trouble to make this for you, so eat up!"

"Well, I want to do that very much, but…she won't let me eat."

"Wh-wwwwh-what did you saaaaaay?!" Renko put her hands on her hips in a display of exaggerated anger. She peered at Ayaka's downcast face. "What the hell, Ayaka?! You love Kyousuke—"

"He's under a starvation sentence."

"…Huh?"

"My big brother made me angry, so I'm making him go without dinner!" Ayaka yelled at Renko, who had not quite grasped the situation. "This has nothing to do with you, Miss Mask, so could you please just leave?!"

However, Renko did not flinch. "Ah, I see. In other words, you're having a little brother-sister quarrel?"

"…That's right. This is punishment for my big brother. I'm teaching him manners! I have to be strict or he'll never learn his lesson—"

"What a waste."

"…What?"

"It's a waste, Ayaka dear. You have a brother complex, and Kyousuke has a sister complex. You want Kyousuke to eat your cooking, and Kyousuke wants to eat it. It's your precious mutual love… What a waste to miss your chance over something so stupid!"

"So…stupid…?"

"Uh-huh. Stupid. Now listen, Ayaka! Cooking class only comes around once every two months. I don't know why you're angry, but it will be a long time till you get another chance to cook for Kyousuke... and for Kyousuke to eat your cooking! That's too bad, isn't it? Even if you make up and regret it later, it'll already be too late!"

"......"

"And the real tragedy is that all this food is going to waste. You went to so much trouble to prepare it, and made it with your truest feelings, and now you won't even let the person you care about the most have any. It's sad. Not getting your true feelings across is sad..." Renko hung her head, looking crestfallen.

The bitterness of unrequited love—Renko understood it all too well, and to see Ayaka stubbornly obstruct her own feelings must have been unbearable.

"Miss Mask?" Ayaka stared at Renko. For a short while, a silence descended, too heavy for words.

With a sigh, Ayaka stood and left the table.

"...Huh?" Renko lifted her face as Ayaka crossed in front of her, and walked over to the cupboards—

"Here, big brother." She set down the small plate and chopsticks in front of Kyousuke's seat.

"...Eh?"

Ayaka ignored her surprised brother, and left the table again. This time she returned with a heaping dish of rice and a hearty bowl of miso soup. Setting them down in front of Kyousuke, Ayaka took her seat. "How long are you going to stand there? Sit down and eat!"

"...Is it okay?"

"If it wasn't, I wouldn't have brought those."

"Seriously?! Th-thank y—"

"But—" Ayaka stopped his mouth with her index finger as he was about to thank her. Her voice was stern, and she stared into Kyousuke's eyes. "This does not mean I'm not angry anymore. It's just that I don't want to waste an opportunity for you to eat my cooking! That's all, so don't get any ideas, okay?"

"...Okay."

"Good. Then, you can eat."

"Thank you for the meal!" Clapping his hands together and taking up his chopsticks, Kyousuke began to eat. First he had a mouthful of miso soup. The flavor of the blended miso filled his mouth. He swallowed it down, savoring the aroma of dashi.

—I've missed this. To Kyousuke, it was the flavor of the everyday life he had lost. Along with the warmth of the food, another warm emotion spread throughout his whole body.

Once he had started moving his chopsticks, there was no stopping them. He ate his meal in a trance. Meat and potato stew, miso-simmered mackerel, fried chicken, rolled omelets, boiled greens—he ate so fast that rice spilled from his mouth. It was so nostalgic he couldn't stand it.

In an instant, his bowl was empty. Faster than Kyousuke could ask, Ayaka had dished up more. "Here you go!"

He accepted the heaping rice bowl with a chiming "thank you!" and quickly resumed scarfing.

Ayaka watched over Kyousuke with a smile as he ravenously wolfed down the food. Renko, Kitou, and Kousaka also stared silently as he ate.

"What a treat!"

He laid his chopsticks down and pressed his hands together in a gesture of gratitude. In less than twenty minutes, Kyousuke had eaten everything. He rubbed his stomach, looking satisfied, as Ayaka filled his cup with barley tea.

"...How was it?"

"It was incredibly delicious!"

"Oh? Tee-hee-hee!" Ayaka looked pleased at Kyousuke's review. Her expression showed a mix of happiness and relief, without the faintest trace of anger.

Kyousuke sipped the cold tea, immersed in lingering joy. "Wooow, I'm happy to be alive... It was so delicious I thought I might die!"

"Tee-hee! You're exaggerating, big brother. But...I really am glad."

"...*Kksshh*..." Renko sighed contently, watching the smiling siblings. Turning to face her gas mask, Kyousuke bowed his head. "Thank you, Renko. Ayaka only let me eat her cooking because you spoke up for me. Seriously, thank you! How can I show my gratitude...?"

"Sure. You can repay me with your body!"

"Uh..."

"*Kksshh.* Just joking. I don't need any thanks, Kyousuke. You looked truly happy when you were eating. Just getting to see you like that is enough. Plus, Ayaka also looked really happy! Watching the two of you, even I felt all warm and fluffy inside." ·

"Renko…"

"GMK…"

"_____"

Ayaka turned away without saying anything.

Renko sighed. "*Kksshh…*" Her voice was full of regret. "But in the end, I couldn't eat Ayaka's cooking, huh? I really wanted to try some, too…but I guess it can't be helped. The food was made for Kyousuke after all. Maybe some other time—"

"Unn!"

Ayaka thrust a cup in front of Renko's mask.

"…Unn?"

Renko tilted her head in confusion.

"Unn!"

Ayaka thrust out the cup once more.

"…Unn?"

"…'Unn' is not an answer!" Ayaka shouted impatiently. Pressing the cup into Renko's hand, she forced her to take it. Then she filled the cup with tea from the kettle.

"Eh?" Renko looked bewildered. "Ayaka…? Ah, umm—"

"Here." Ayaka finished pouring the tea and turned away again. "I won't give you any of my cooking," she said bluntly, "but I guess it'd be okay to give you some of the tea I brewed. You can drink with that mask on, right? I hope you appreciate it…"

"A-Ayaka…!" Renko sounded deeply moved, and quickly prepared her straw tube. She stuck the end opposite the one attached to the cheek of her gas mask into the cup, and sucked it up with a long *sluuurp*. "Delicious! This tea is incredibly delicious! *Slurp… slurp…*"

"Thanks, but…it's just ordinary barley tea."

"Seconds, pleeeeeease!"

"Absolutely not. You only get one cup."

"*Kksshh…*"

"Tee-hee!"

Renko looked dejected as the empty cup was snatched away. Ayaka grinned and filled her own cup with tea. Kyousuke, too, felt a smile spread across his face, happy that the exchange had been so calm. Slowly, steadily, little by little, the distance between the two of them was beginning to close.

If this kept up, Ayaka was sure to become good friends with everyone.

X   X   X

"No way."

Ayaka pursed her lips in flat denial. They had finished washing the dishes a short while ago. Now Kyousuke brought Maina over, hoping the two of them could reconcile before the other groups finished cooking, but Ayaka had obstinately refused.

"C'mon, don't be like that... Please try to get along... *Okay?*"

"No way. Nowaynowaynowaynoway! Absolutely not!" Ayaka shook her head furiously "No means no!"

Maina's eyes filled with tears. "Ohh..."

Eiri rubbed her forehead. "Eh."

Renko looked highly perplexed. "Oh my."

"Why do you hate the idea so much...?"

"I told you, Crafty Cat is too cunning."

"Cunning... What about her is so cunning?"

"Her everything."

Ayaka angrily puffed out her cheeks.

"...Everything?"

Kyousuke sounded crestfallen.

"Geez, why are you sticking up for her?! Are you a Crafty Cat fan?"

"...What do you mean by 'fan'?"

"I mean, is she your favorite? Hey, actually, Bro..." Ayaka stood up and glared at Maina, Eiri, and Renko in turn. "Big brother, out of these three girls, who do you like the best?"

"......?!"

All three girls reacted decisively...and dramatically.

Maina shrieked, and leaped out of her seat: "Eeeeee?!"

Eiri blushed furiously: "Uh..."

Renko recoiled: "'L-like the beeeeeest'?!"

Kyousuke's mouth hung open, and he looked back into Ayaka's eyes. "Just what are you talking about?"

"Tee-hee! I was just a little curious. Besides, you all want to know, too, right?" Ayaka shot the other girls a smile.

Maina's eyes began filling with tears. "Oh my, oh dear. I'm, I'm... curious, but also scared...oh no..."

Eiri fiddled absently with her hair. "...Tch, like I care about something so stupid. Are you an idiot?"

Renko pressed in on Kyousuke. "I am! I am! I'm really curious! Of course it's me, right, Kyousuke?!"

Sweat broke out on Kyousuke's forehead. "U-uuummm..."

"Look, you have to answer honestly. Who is it? Who do you like the best, big brother?"

"Uh......th-that's......well..."

Kyousuke gulped audibly. Each gaze was focused on him like a laser. Closing his eyes, he took a deep breath to compose his thoughts.

"...All of you!"

"_____"

Time seemed to stop with his answer. The light went out of Maina's and Eiri's eyes. The face behind the gas mask was also silent.

"What? I answered you, didn't I?" asked Kyousuke, baffled. "I said I like all of you..."

"...A three-way..." Renko growled. Her voice was low and difficult to hear.

"Huh?"

"A three-waaaaaaaaaaaaayyy! All of us? ...What the hell do you mean, 'all of uuuuuusss?!' Stupiiiiiiiiiiiid! Stupidstupidstupidstupid! Kyousuke, you idiooooooot!"

Renko continued shouting while beating him over and over.

"Ehh?!"

Kyousuke's wide-eyed expression was met with a piercing, icy stare from Eiri. "...The worst. I was the idiot for expecting anything of this loser."

"Kyo-Kyousuke...Japan is not a polygamous country!" Even Maina had turned an accusatory eye on him.

"Just a...wait, wait, you've got it wrong! When I said 'all of you,' I didn't mean it like that! I mean, I like you, but in a different way... To me you three are all dear friends, and I can't assign you ranks or anything! That's why—"

"Well, what if your little sister enters the running?" Ayaka asked gently, peering up at Kyousuke's face earnestly. "Crafty Cat, Miss Akabonehead, Miss Mask, and Ayaka. If it's among these four people, who does my big brother like the best?"

"...Uhhh..." Kyousuke floundered for a reply. Ayaka was, without a doubt, the most important person in all the world. However, he was reluctant to place her in the same category as Renko and the others. They were all still his dear friends, and if possible, he wanted to avoid hurting anybody. He really had no idea how to answer. "A...all of you!"

"_____"

Time seemed to freeze again as Kyousuke repeated his answer.

Ayaka's eyes grew dark.

"...Idiot," Eiri groaned, holding her forehead.

"Ah, no, that is..." Kyousuke quickly followed up. "I like you, Ayaka, truly! I love you most in all the world! But I can't compare you to these girls. I mean, there's no comparison—I mean...it's not like I can rank you or anything, right? Like an evaluation on an absolute scale, and not a comparative assessment. Something like that—"

"Okay. I understand very well, big brother."

"Ohh, really?!"

"Yes. I understand veeeeeeeeeeeeery well that you want to make me angry! Why, I should have let you starve after all!" Hanging her head, Ayaka clenched her fists.

"......Eh?" Kyousuke tried to read his little sister's expression.

"—*Spit it out!*"

Ayaka's fist struck Kyousuke's stomach, hard.

"Guh—?!"

He crumbled under the surprise assault while Maina and the others screamed.

"Kyousuke?!"

"Kyousuke!"

"Ayaka?!"

Kyousuke felt dreadful waves of nausea wash over his extremely full stomach. As he doubled over, trying to control his agonized innards, he heard a bone-chilling voice from above.

"Spit it out, big brother! If you haven't learned your lesson, then all of the food you just ate…I'm confiscating it!"

"A…ya…ka…?" Her voice, and the shock of her striking him for the first time, hit Kyousuke much harder than her fist. —*Why? How come?*

Ayaka looked down at him with eyes so dark and gloomy that Kyousuke almost forgot the pain. "I love you the most, big brother, so why won't you say that you love me the most? Aren't I that important to you?"

"……"

"Hey, why won't you answer me? You won't answer because you can't answer, isn't that right? And the reason why you can't answer is…in other words…I'm right? And if I'm right, then…yeah, spit it out! Here, I'll make you confess—"

Ayaka prepared to kick Kyousuke in the stomach.

"Stop it!" Forcing herself between them, Renko pushed Ayaka.

The girl stared at Renko's gas mask with hard eyes. "…What is it?"

"Don't ask me 'what is it?' Do you even understand what you've done? Look at Kyousuke! He's not in any condition to speak."

"_____"

Moved by Renko's heart-wrenching tone, Ayaka turned to look at Kyousuke, who was still sweating and holding his stomach, eyes vacant.

"……Ah." As she gazed at her older brother, Ayaka's eyes seemed to clear. She crouched down in a panic, suddenly afraid for his well-being. "Big brother!"

Her dry eyes quickly became wet with tears, and swam restlessly through space. "Ah, aaah…s-sorry…I'm sorry!! R-really sorry…the blood rushed to my head, and then suddenly…I'm sorry! Really, really sorry! Ohh… does it hurt? Of course it hurts…ah…wh-wwwwh-what do we do… What did I do to you… Sorry… I'm sorry, big brother! Oh, ohh…I'm sorry… I'msorryI'msorryI'msorryI'msorryI'msorryI'msorryI'msorry I'msorryI'msorryI'msorryI'msorryI'msorryI'msorryI'msorry I'msorryI'msorryI'msorryI'msorryI'msorryI'msorryI'msorry—"

"Ayaka."

A hand came to rest on Ayaka's head as she continued her frantic apologies. Surprised, she lifted her face to see Kyousuke forcing a pained smile.

"It's all right. You don't need to apologize…"

"Big brother…"

Gazing at her tear-streaked face, Kyousuke tousled her hair. "…I'm not worried about my body. Taking one punch to the stomach won't kill me. So don't worry so much."

"Big brother, um…y-you're not mad…?"

"I'm not mad. What do I have to be mad about? I should be sorry, instead of you… It was my fault for making you that angry. As your inadequate older brother, I'm truly sorry…"

"……?!"

Ayaka buried her face in Kyousuke's chest as if to hide. "…You didn't do anything wrong," she mumbled, mournful.

Watching Kyousuke gently stroke Ayaka's back, Renko sighed. "…*Kksshh.*"

Eiri and Maina also looked exhausted, but at least, for the moment, the situation showed some signs of resolution.

—It started the following day.

Ayaka seemed even more infatuated with Kyousuke than before.

Can You Feel My Heart?

THE WORLD WILL COME TO NOTHING

QUESTION FOUR

Q: What is your target rank on the final exams?
Nothing. I don't have any goals or anything.

Q: What are your strongest and weakest subjects?
None. I don't have any strong subjects or anything.

Q: If you are granted parole, what do you want to do?
Nothing. I don't want to go on a shopping date or anything.
I don't need cute clothes or anything.
I don't want to eat sweets or anything.
I don't want to cuddle a stuffed animal or anything!

Q: Tell us about your enthusiasm for the tests!
It's pointless...

"…Huh? Big brother, where are you going?"

It was the second period break. At the sound of the chime, Kyousuke stood. "To the bathroom," he announced.

"Is that so?" Ayaka remarked casually. "Then I'll go, too!"

Kyousuke's heart sank at her response. He had been afraid of this. Two days had passed since cooking class, and Ayaka's fawning had grown more and more oppressive.

She held his hand whenever they walked together, constantly said "I love you," smothered him in embraces, linked arms whenever they sat together, badgered him to feed her during meals, and refused to speak to anyone else.

It was exactly like when she had first arrived. She refused to be separated from his side even for a moment, and yesterday she had even started to accompany him to the boys' toilets. It wouldn't have been so bad if she'd just waited outside, but she insisted on even coming in with him. Her cheerful yammering made trying to do his business very uncomfortable. She'd even tried to excuse her behavior, saying, "I'm checking your health through your pee, big brother!" She could have at least considered how he might feel getting a urinalysis from his *sister*.

"Let me see…" Kyousuke muttered, sounding defeated. The past two days had been utterly exhausting. She'd clung to him the whole time. Kyousuke still loved the girl, but all the same he felt hopelessly depressed. *It'll be embarrassing if she comes inside with me again, so just to be sure—*

"You're also, um…using the bathroom?"

"Nope," she answered indifferently. "I'm just coming with you!"

"O-oh…I see."

Kyousuke didn't want to be cruel, but he had to put an end to this here.

"Sorry, Ayaka, but if that's the case, could I get you to wait in the classroom?"

"Why?"

"Why…? Well…it-it's embarrassing."

"…You hate it?"

"Honestly, I'm not happy about it."

"……"

Ayaka's expression grew severe, her eyes downcast in contemplation. Seeming to reach a quick conclusion, she then smiled and nodded. "I get it! If you don't like it, I'll stop. I'll be a good girl and wait here, okay?"

"Ah, sorry… I'll come right back."

"Sure, off you go! Is it a number two?"

"……It's a number one."

Kyousuke left the classroom wishing she hadn't made a point of asking. He cut across the hallway, dodging groups of loitering murderers, and entered the nearest boys' toilets.

Though she had agreed to the separation, he was reluctant to leave Ayaka on her own. Eiri and Maina were in the classroom with her, but it could still be a problem if any troublesome classmates tried to give her a hard time.

Kyousuke quickly relieved himself, and when he had finished washing his hands—

"Wait right there."

There was a girl standing in the hallway immediately outside the boys' toilets, listlessly fiddling with the tip of her ponytail.

"......Eiri? Weren't you in the classroom?"

"I followed you."

"Eh?! Don't tell me you're also interested in my...?!"

"...What? No! It's nothing like that. Are you trying to get me to cut you?"

Kyousuke felt her stare pierce his abdomen. He cringed, afraid for many reasons.

Eiri clicked her tongue, "...Tch," and stepped away from the wall. She walked toward him boldly. "I want to talk to you a bit about your little shadow."

"......Eh?"

Dragging Kyousuke into a corner of the hallway, she lowered her voice. "Tell me, you...what do you think about her?"

"What do you mean? What? Of course she's important to me, but—"

"That's not what I mean. I'm talking about her behavior."

"Uh..."

Ayaka had been awfully aggressive and thorny since arriving at the Institution. And yet, she'd been overly sweet to Kyousuke...

However, Ayaka had never acted like that before.

She had always been courteous and good-mannered, and had a reputation as a "good girl" in their neighborhood. She was an honors student, the polar opposite of her infamous brother, and he was immensely proud of his almost-too-perfect little sister. Their sibling relationship had always been good, and she had never been inappropriately clingy or acted so absurdly selfish. But now Ayaka was—

"...It's obvious, isn't it?"

Eiri was shocked at Kyousuke's lack of understanding for his sister's change in behavior. "Have you forgotten what kind of place this is? It's an academy for murderers. Anybody who *could* carry on normally after being thrown into a place like this would have to be *pretty strange*."

"Uh......"

Eiri spoke the truth. Still, a sense of vague discomfort settled deep in Kyousuke's chest, as though he had forgotten something terribly important, or mistaken it for something else—

"Maybe..." Eiri paused before continuing, "...it's uneasiness. Feeling like you can't let your guard down around anyone, and that every last person could be an enemy… I was the same way myself, so I kind of understand it. And Ayaka isn't even an experienced murderer… I get why she feels like she has to be pointlessly aggressive, to keep from getting picked on. But she doesn't have to be that way with you, right?"

A critical light glimmered in Eiri's piercing, rust-red eyes. "You're the only one, a blood relative whom she can trust with all her heart. You're her family, someone she wanted to see so badly that she was willing to attempt murder. You've got to forgive her for fawning over you a little too much…because you're the only person here whom she can trust. That's what I think whenever I see her in the dorms."

"…Ayaka in the dorms?"

"Yeah. She's quiet, like a completely different person! I think it's because you're not there, but she's silent the whole time. Even when Maina and I talk to her, she's curt. And it seems like she has no intention of reaching out on her own. On the first day, she asked us things like 'Are you really his friends?' and 'How did you get close to him?' and 'What do you think of him?'…She only asked about things that had to do with you. And she always seems to be on her guard."

"……Seriously?"

"Seriously. That's why, Kyousuke…take better care of that girl! We're fine for now, but—remember what she asked you during cooking class? 'Who do you love the best?' You were probably thinking of our feelings, but…don't worry about that. For now, you think only about her. She has no one to rely on except for you, and if you don't make her your number one priority, she'll be too anxious."

"Eiri…"

"I believe the two of us can become close friends as well, and I can open up to her. But you know, I think it's still too soon. First, you need to be there for her, as her 'big brother.' That's what I wanted to tell you." As she finished speaking, Eiri swept her hair back, scratched her cheek, and looked away.

Kyousuke was pleasantly surprised. She was much more concerned about Ayaka than he had thought; he wouldn't have to go out of his way to intervene. Eiri would sort things out with Ayaka on her own.

"…That's right," Kyousuke agreed. "Supporting my sister should be my first priority. Thanks, Eiri. Really, thank you for worrying about Ayaka."

"Sure. You should think only about her well-being. Because we're all worried about her, too. So in other words, um…f-fawn over her more, okay?"

Eiri's cheeks flushed. Playing with the end of her ponytail, she pouted her lips into a sulk. Her language was blunt, but every word and action showed her concern.

Looking at her like that, Kyousuke's heart filled with gratitude and joy. "Ohh! Thank you, Eiriiiiii!" Kyousuke cheerfully rubbed his friend's head with both hands.

"Hyaaaaaah?!" she shouted hysterically. Her whole body stiffened. "Wha-wwwwha-what…wh-what are you…wwwh-what—"

"—Huh?! S-sorry…" Regaining his composure, Kyousuke pulled away in a panic. "I didn't mean to!"

Her hair disheveled, Eiri was blank with shock, and her mouth gaped appropriately. "……D-didn't mean to…didn't mean…" Her shoulders trembled slightly, and her face turned a very bright shade of red.

And then, her astonishment gave way to anger: "Y-you…! Even if you're joking, don't get carried away!!"

"Uh?! Wow, I'm really sorry…but look, earlier you said, 'fawn over her'—"

"I didn't mean physically, you idiot! Lecher! Pervert!" Eiri frantically combed her fingers through her hair as she piled on the abuse.

She took a step away from Kyousuke and hung her head. "I thought my heart was gonna stop…" she muttered. "E-even *I* wasn't ready for that…"

"…Huh? What are you mumbling about?"

"I said you'd be better off dead!"

"D-don't get angry… I said I was sorry. I was just so happy…"

"…Hmph. Save that stuff for the girl." Eiri sighed, looking at him with narrowed eyes. She brushed her hair back again in irritation. "An-y-way! That's all I had to say. Hurry up and get back to her. She's probably starting to miss you by now."

"…Yeah, you're right. But seriously…thank you, Eiri."

"Don't mention it." She waved nonchalantly and walked away, her usual careless attitude returned.

And yet, the last that Kyousuke saw of her, Eiri was still smiling slightly.

X   X   X

"You took forever, big brother! It wasn't a number one, was it?"

Ayaka greeted Kyousuke cheerfully when he returned to the classroom. Maina had also stayed behind with her, but Renko, who had been talking with them before, was now gone. Before he entered the classroom, Kyousuke had peeked in and glimpsed the two of them staring silently at the floor.

Kyousuke recalled what Eiri had just said: When he wasn't around, Ayaka was quiet and wouldn't reach out to anyone. It seemed the relationship between her and Maina had yet to really improve. Kyousuke tried to suppress his feelings of disappointment. *Right now I have to think only about Ayaka.*

"Oh, sorry. I don't know why, but for some reason my stomach suddenly didn't feel so great…" Kyousuke had separated from Eiri in front of the boys' toilets and returned to the classroom alone. "…Wh-what is it?"

Ayaka stared intently at Kyousuke as he tried to explain his long absence. "Suspicious…"

"Eh?"

"Did you really go to the bathroom?"

"O-of course I did…"

"Hmmm…" Glancing at the empty seat two desks over, Ayaka quickly stood. Facing Kyousuke, she leaned in close and sniffed him. "…You stink."

"Eh?!"

Ayaka began to sniff Kyousuke's whole body, frowning. Stomach, chest, shoulders, both arms… She dragged her nose over every part, sniffing and smelling.

Kyousuke was baffled by this sudden and eccentric behavior. "Just a… What are you—?"

"…Again. It's Miss Akabonehead again."

"Huh?"

"Miss Akabonehead's scent is all over you, big brother!" Reaching the ends of his arms, Ayaka lifted her face and glared at Kyousuke. Burning anger roiled in her big black eyes. "Did something happen between you two?"

"N-no..."

"Liar."

"It's not a lie!"

"Oh, well, I guess it was nothing, then."

"Of course! I just went to the bathroom—"

"Don't liiiiiiiiiiiiiiiiiiiiiiiiiiiiiiiieeeeeeeeeeeeeeeeeeee!"

The classroom fell silent at the volume and intensity of Ayaka's voice. Between her fingers she held a long, fine thread—a strand of rust-red-colored hair.

Ayaka thrust the piece of "evidence" under Kyousuke's nose. "Big brother! You had this stuck to your shoulder!"

Her voice was gentle and kind, and she smiled sweetly.

But her eyes were not smiling, and the light had gone out of them. "This is Miss Akabonehead's hair, isn't it? Why is *filth* like this stuck to you? I don't remember seeing it before you went to the toilet, though... Tee-hee! Strange, isn't it...? Definitely strange! Something definitely did happen, didn't it iiiiiit, big broooooother?!"

Ayaka's smiling face completely changed. With a shrill cry, she kicked a nearby desk, sending it flying. Kyousuke was completely overwhelmed. He failed to respond.

Ayaka grabbed his collar and pulled him toward her, looking like she might burst into tears at any moment.

"You're so cruel! Why do you tell lies, big brother? Why do you hide things from your little sister? Why do you always keep quiet? You're cruel, big brother, too cruel... Your sister trusts in you, big brother, and despite that, you...waaaaaahhh. How come? Why?! Whywhywhywhy do you—"

"...Huh? What happened?" Eiri asked, interrupting Ayaka's tantrum. Standing in the doorway, she surveyed the classroom, which had been seized by a strange atmosphere.

"_____"

Ayaka stopped. Slowly, she let go of Kyousuke's collar. Very slowly, she turned to face Eiri.

"All right, you bastards! The bell's gonna ring soon! Take your seats!" Their petite homeroom teacher stepped out from behind Eiri.

"...Ah." Ayaka's hand stopped midway across the desk. She had been reaching for a pencil cup with mechanical pencils jutting out of it.

Kurumiya scowled. "Hmm...? What is it, Miss Kamiya? You look like you've seen a ghost."

"No, no! It's nothing. Just a little lovers' quarrel..." Withdrawing her arm, Ayaka waved dismissively.

She was back to acting like a normal little sister. The change was too fast. It was impossible to keep up.

Eiri stood blinking, looking confused.

"Hmm..." Kurumiya put her hand on her chin. "Well, whatever. Hey, you pig-bastards, in your seats, now! This period there will be a pop quiz covering everything that will be on the end-of-term exams. You idiots better take it seriously."

A chime signaling the start of class rang out as Kurumiya took her place at the lectern. With another inquisitive glance at the two siblings, Eiri returned to her seat. Ayaka smiled meaningfully, and Kyousuke dropped his gaze, unable to do anything but hang his head in shame.

Their scores on the pop quiz were pitiful.

X   X   X

"Miss Akabonehead, what did you do with my big brother during the break?"

Ayaka had approached Eiri's desk as soon as class had ended. Eiri, who had actually been taking notes for once, stopped writing, put down her pen, and looked up at Ayaka with a friendly smile.

Several moments passed in silence, in which Eiri knit her eyebrows, looking puzzled.

"...When we passed by each other in the hallway, we just talked a little," she answered. "That's all!"

She had also answered Ayaka's unspoken question. Eiri quickly returned to her writing.

—Bam! Ayaka slammed a hand down on Eiri's pen. "That's a lie, isn't it?"

"…What? No it isn't." Eiri scowled at the interruption.

Ayaka presented her "evidence"—in her free hand, she held between her thumb and forefinger a long strand of rust-red hair.

"This belongs to you, doesn't it, Miss Akabonehead? It was stuck to my big brother's shoulder."

"……." Eiri glanced at Kyousuke. "Oh really? I wonder when it got stuck. How mysterious."

"Isn't iiiiiit? It's sooo mysteeeeeerious. Yes, very mysterious indeed…" Ayaka's temple twitched in anger. Waving the strand of hair back and forth, her tone grew firm. "Before my big brother went to the bathroom, he did not have anything like this stuck to him, I'm sure! Is talking with someone, just a little bit, enough to get your hair all over them? It isn't, iiiiiiiisss iiiiiiiiit?!"

"…It must have stuck to him when we passed each other in the hallway."

"Ah, I see…not! There's no way that's true!! Unless…Miss Akabonehead, are you losing your hair? I'm going to change your name to Miss Akabaldy!"

"…And if you do?"

"I won't! Don't change the subject!"

"You're the one who brought it up…" Eiri grumbled. She sounded fed up with the whole affair.

Ayaka showed no intention of letting up. She leaned in on Eiri suspiciously, pressing her for answers. "Even if that were the case, he still smells like you."

"…Smells?"

"Smells. Your scent is all over my big brother's chest—" Ayaka sniffed the air and grimaced. "Stinky! You smell just like a female pig!"

"…What did you say?"

"Oh, sorry. Forget 'just like'…you are a pig! A big stiiiiiiiiiiinky sow!" Ayaka held her nose and pantomimed fanning herself.

"……Tch." Eiri clicked her tongue.

Kyousuke could not stand to watch any longer. "Hey now, that's taking it too far!" he rebuked. "Just let it go."

"Boo… Big brother…are you taking Miss Akabonehead's side instead of your own little sister's?"

"…Uhhh…th-that's—" Kyousuke trailed off as Ayaka stared at him sadly and Eiri gave him a critical look. Recalling what she had said during the break, Kyousuke shook his head. "...No, I'm on your side. Of course I am!"

"Big brother..."

Ayaka seemed to be pleased by his reassuring answer. Her miserable expression changed to a broad smile in an instant.

"—Well, then, why are you really lying to me?"

".......Eh?"

"No, not 'eh?' You told me a lie. You said that nothing happened between you and Miss Akabonehead. Why would you lie to me if you're really on my side, big brother? Why would you keep secrets with Miss Akabonehead? You're contradicting yourself, aren't you? It sure is puzzling."

Throughout her verbal assault, Ayaka had never stopped smiling. Sweat broke out on Kyousuke's back. "Uh, ummm...that's, well—"

"I beg your pardon."

A familiar voice rang out from the front of the classroom. A female student was peeking her head in through the doorway. The beautiful, Western-looking girl had honey-colored hair and emerald eyes.

"Miss Shamaya? What brings you to a place like this...?"

"Oh-ho-ho! I'm out on my midday patrol of the school. How do you do, everyone?" Shamaya leaned around the door and waved. She wore a yellow armband that read "Public Morals Committee." Patrol or no, this was the first time they had caught sight of Shamaya—or any of the upperclassmen—in the old school building. It was obvious that she had some other purpose for being there.

"...She came out, huh?" Ayaka said, sounding annoyed. "That bitch..."

Shamaya continued smiling. "It's been a long time, little sister. Your name was...Ayaka, yes?"

"Don't address me so casually, please. It fouls my ears."

"Ah, as ever you are an unsparing one... Well, that is fine." Shamaya cleared her throat and looked around the room. "It appears that Miss

Hikawa is not present...very good, very good! I shall finish my business without delay. Oh-ho-ho-ho-ho!" Her eyes shone as she smiled disarmingly.

The previous week, Shamaya had suffered through a terrible ordeal thanks to Kyousuke and the others. They still had not cleared up the misunderstanding between them, and she probably still thought—wrongly—that he hated her.

—There was no way that a genuine psychopath like Shamaya would leave it at that.

"Kyousuke dear. I've been thinking about a lot of things since that incident! Ever since I found out that you dislike me, night after night I've been thinking... I considered a gracious surrender, but...I cannot give up... I've made up my mind. Even if I have to be a little pushy, I promise that I will get my hands on Kyousuke! You may think me selfish, and you may find me annoying, but...in my own way, I must pursue my darling Kyousuke!"

As she finished, Shamaya stepped out from behind the door.

Held in one of her arms was a hard, white-lacquered case. It was rectangular, like the cases used to store musical instruments, and the surface was decorated with gold inlay.

"Ah!" Ayaka exclaimed the moment she laid eyes upon that case.

"Oh no—" Eiri went completely pale. She turned to yell at Kyousuke and the others in an urgent voice.

"It's a gun! Run!"

"......?!" Their classmates froze in place.

Shamaya set the case on the floor and moved to undo the clasp.

"Eeek!!" Maina shrieked and dove under her desk.

Eiri pulled Ayaka close, as if to protect her.

Kyousuke, sensing danger, leaped to his feet, pushed aside his desk, and burst into a sprint. "Hyeaaaaaaaaah!" He tackled Shamaya just as she was about to reach the gun.

"Kyaaah! Mon Dieu!!" Shamaya kicked and struggled as Kyousuke forced her hands behind her back. "Ohh, Kyousuke darling...how very intense! Please don't be so violent...at least at first! And what's more, in public like this…my goodness. I am a closet masochist, but… this is too much, too soon! We haven't even joined hands yet! And yet you intend to join our other parts, oh myyy!!"

"What the hell are you going on about?! You were about to shoot us!"

"…Hm? Shoot you? Whatever are *you* talking about, Kyousuke darling?"

"What do you mean, what am I…?" Kyousuke looked flabbergasted. "The gun—obviously!" He pointed to the case.

"Ahh." Shamaya nodded. "But you've got it all wrong. This is a case for a gun, yes, but I currently use it as a lunch box. I simply could not find a better container."

The inside of the case was indeed filled—not with a gun—but instead with gourmet food. One half was stuffed with an assortment of sandwiches, and the other with various side dishes like fried chicken, rolled omelets, meatballs, and wieners, all arranged artfully in neat compartments.

"……"

The tense atmosphere subsided, and a subdued silence descended upon the room.

Shamaya twisted around and looked embarrassed. "Ah, um…Kyousuke dear? If we've cleared up the misunderstanding, I'll ask you to release me, please. Pressing closely against you like this, I…I don't think I can hold back! Ha-ha! My dear Kyousuke's hands…they're so rugged and they feel so good… Ohhh, Kyousuke…! Feast not on the boxed lunch, but on your dear Shamaya—"

"I'll pass."

"…Aw."

Kyousuke quickly stepped aside as Shamaya stood up, looking disappointed. Their classmates, realizing that it had all been a misunderstanding, grumbled and complained as they went back to what they had been doing. "What the hell…?" "You scared me." "I wasn't scaaared!" "It's a gun, run! *Not!* Geez…" "Die!" "This is why she has small boobs…"

Ayaka laughed. "Tee-hee! How embarrassing, Miss Akabonehead! What a stupid mistake!"

"Sh-shut up! It's because she was acting weird…"

"Your face is turning reeeeeed! Tee-hee! And anyway, how long are you going to cling to me?! Your dirty sow stink is gonna rub off on me! Get away!"

Eiri, who had been holding Ayaka in a protective embrace, grunted, "Kyuh?!" as Ayaka pushed her away.

Maina poked her head out from under her desk and looked around. "M-misfire…?"

"Oh-ho-ho! I do beg your pardon for the panic. I made a bento box for you all! Living on table scraps cannot be good for your health. It's probably none of my business, but in order to impress my darling Kyousuke—or rather…I mean, in order to make all of you very happy, I worked through the night preparing it!"

Shamaya presented the case to Kyousuke. The side dishes, packed in tightly with no space to spare, would have been more than enough for the four of them.

"Miss Shamaya, you made all of this by yourself…?"

"Yes, of course I did! Cooking is my forte. It looks good, of course, but I can promise you it also tastes great. I carefully selected each ingredient. The meat was strangled to death during the night, and only sliced up at the last minute! It's veeeeeery fresh."

"It's not human meat, is it?"

"……Of course not."

"That was a long pause, wasn't it?! When you say it, it doesn't sound like a joke, you know!"

"Oh-ho-ho-ho-ho! There's no need for concern, I promise you. It's not human meat, it's chicken. I borrowed a chicken from the coop in Purgatory Park. It put up quite a struggle, so I had a dreadful time of it…"

"No way, that's ridiculous. If anyone found out, you would get in real trouble, wouldn't you…?"

"Indeed. And, in fact, I have already been discovered. Not long ago I received a summons. It said, 'You, too, shall follow the same fate as the chicken.' Miss Mizuchi, who is the advisor to the Public Morals Committee, is famous for being the kindest teacher at the academy, but she is also famous for being the scariest when angered. After the previous scandal, I was beaten, viciously, for three days and three nights. I must have passed out nearly a thousand times."

That's sick! It's amazing she even survived.

…And despite that experience, she was back to causing trouble, with no concern for her own safety.

"Oh-ho-ho!" Shamaya laughed, ignoring Kyousuke's concerned expression. "This time I'm likely to die! But it doesn't matter! If I can make my darling Kyousuke happy, I will be satisfied… After all, I am so in love with Kyousuke! I've made up my mind—I am ready to give my life in the name of love! So please eat, Kyousuke darling! Eat this meal, made by my own two hands and filled with my love! If you do that, I can die peacefully…" Shamaya's eyes sparkled as she held out the case.

Kyousuke took a firm hold so that she would not drop it. It was heavier than he would have guessed. It must have weighed heavy in her arms and on her heart.

"…Th-thank you."

"I should thank you! Ah, now at last I am prepared to meet my certain death… Adieu, Kyousuke darling. If by chance we meet again, please embrace me with all your strength! That alone will be enough, so—"

Wham!

The case sailed through the air. The handmade lunch box, knocked from Kyousuke's grasp, fell to the floor, spilling its magnificent contents everywhere.

"_____"

Shamaya froze. Kyousuke held his breath.

It had been so sudden. They did not understand what had happened.

The lunch box was a wreck of scattered sandwiches and side dishes.

Kyousuke and Shamaya stared, unmoving.

"Good grief! Don't let her fool you, big brother. Miss Bitch here is the infamous Killer Queen, after all. Another moment more and you could have died! What would we do if it was full of poison or something? Sheesh…it's dangerous, dangerous!"

Sighing, Ayaka wiped away cold sweat.

She had cut in from the side and thrown the case over.

"What are you…"

"I told you before! I protected you from Miss Bitch's evil influence. You should be more careful, big brother!" Ayaka glared at Kyousuke indignantly. "Even with a beautiful girl…if you're careless, that's when you'll die, just like that! Do you understand?!"

"Th-there's no way that such a thing—"

A groan escaped from Shamaya's mouth. "……not…said…"

"What?"

At the same time that Ayaka looked in her direction, Shamaya also looked up at her. "It is not filled with poison or anything! As I said before, there was one subtle seasoning that I used in my cooking. It was nothing but love and XXX!"

…Just then, didn't she add some dangerous word after "love"?

"Hang on!" Ayaka closed in on Shamaya. "Don't put your weird ingredients in food you're going to give to my big brother! That in itself is a poison, isn't it? If he ate food polluted by your love, my big brother would be polluted just the same! You stupid bitch!"

"S-stupid bi…why…you! How dare you speak to me in such a way?! And after ruining the meal that I worked so hard to prepare?! I tolerated you before because you are my darling Kyousuke's younger sister, but you have reached the very limit of my patience! Now I'm angry… I demand an apology, Miss Ayaka!"

"Absolutely not. You should be the one apologizing."

"Whaaat?! Why ever should I apologize?!"

"Because you tried to poison my big brother! Why are you playing dumb?"

"I am not playing dumb! There is not the slightest bit of poison—"

"Then you eat it."

"……Wha?"

Pointing at the lunch box, which still sat upended on the floor, Ayaka smiled cheerfully. "Let me see you eat it yourself. And then if nothing happens to you, I'll admit that it's not poisoned. I'll admit that you weren't trying to kill my big brother."

The expression disappeared from Shamaya's face. "…Put that food in my mouth, you say?"

"That's right. It got a little dirty, but it was filthy with your love to begin with, so it's all the same, isn't it? Unless, as we thought, it's got poison in it—is that why you won't eat it?"

"———"

The light disappeared from Shamaya's eyes. As Ayaka snickered with laughter, she took a step closer. "I understand."

"......Eh?"

"If such an indignity will clear my name, I shall do it gladly! Between my love for Kyousuke and my silly pride...there is no contest!" Shamaya knelt, pinching her skirt behind her knees and tucking her honey-colored hair behind her ear. Without hesitation, she picked up a piece of fried chicken. As Ayaka watched, astonished, she daintily brushed away some of the dirt. "Well, then, here I go—"

"I'll take that."

—*Yoink*. A hand reach down from above and snatched the fried chicken.

"Aaah?!" Shamaya and Ayaka shouted in unison as the thief sampled the stolen chicken.

"Oh, that's good."

"......Kyousuke...darling?"

Shamaya was frozen in shock.

Kyousuke grinned as he finished eating. "You're a really good cook, eh? That was delicious, even cold. Thank you so much for the food!"

"Kyo-Kyousuke darling...I thought you hated me?"

"I don't hate you! I was trying to tell you that, but...we left off at a weird place last time, I know, and it caused a bit of a misunderstanding. I'm really sorry. Oh, and also, my sister is—"

"Think nothing of it!" Shamaya interrupted. "You don't need to apologize." She got to her feet. "Just hearing you call my cooking delicious...and saying that you don't hate me...is *more than* more than enough. Oh-ho-ho!" Raising a hand to her chest, Shamaya wore a joyful expression. It was the look of a maiden in love, hardly appropriate for the Killer Queen.

"Miss Shamaya..."

Despite his better judgment, Kyousuke was charmed.

"_____"

Throughout their conversation, Ayaka had been standing, head hung low, wearing an expression that said that at any moment she could explode into violence...

If that happened, there was no way Kyousuke could take Ayaka's side.

X   X   X

Shamaya collected her case and left, saying, "I've been summoned to the discipline room."

Before cleaning up the food that was on the floor, Kyousuke turned to face Ayaka. She had kept her mouth shut to the end, even after Shamaya had left the room, and still stood there, head hanging low.

"...Hey, Ayaka." Kyousuke had planned to hold back, but he couldn't stop himself from speaking in a serious tone. "No matter how you look at it, you said too much, you went too far. I understand that you're angry and suspicious because everyone here is a murderer, but you need to be a little more...ummm...there's a problem with how you say things. That kind of abuse would make anyone feel angry and hurt. They may be murderers, but they're people just like us. Do you understand, Ayaka?"

"_____"

Ayaka did not respond.

Annoyance rose within Kyousuke. He put his hands on both her shoulders, and spoke sternly. "It's not just Miss Shamaya... You act like this toward Eiri and Maina, too. I understand feeling uneasy when you've been thrown into a place like this. I also understand how hard it is to trust a murderer. And I understand that it really bothers you when I get along with people like that. But listen, Ayaka. If you keep acting so hostile, you'll provoke a response from the people around you...and sooner or later no one is going to come near you! You'll be just like I was on the outside—"

"...un...sta...any..."

"Huh?"

"Big brother, you don't understand anything!"

Ayaka brushed Kyousuke's hands away. Her voice was shrill as she continued hysterically. "The reasons why I feel uneasy, and the reasons I can't start liking those people, and the reasons why I'm angry, every one of them! You don't understand anything, even the tiniest biiiiiiiiiiiit!!" Ayaka screamed, clawing at her hair. She looked like a child throwing a temper tantrum.

Kyousuke honestly had no idea what was making her so upset, and was getting frustrated. *I've been with her this whole time, but...* The answer remained just beyond his grasp. "I don't get it, Ayaka! I don't understand why you're so angry! Can't you just explain it to me clearly? If you tell me, maybe I can—"

"So if I don't tell you, you won't understand?" Ayaka looked at Kyousuke with disappointment in her eyes. "...Fine, then." Sulking, she turned away in a huff.

Kyousuke finally threw down his hands in exasperation. "What do you mean by 'fine'?! If you have something you want to say, you should say it."

"No."

"...Say it."

"No!"

"Say it, I said!"

"No way."

"I told you to say it!!"

"No waaay!"

Kyousuke obstinately repeated the demand, and Ayaka stubbornly refused to answer. The two of them stood glaring at each other, before a hand pushed them apart.

"You two are getting too intense."

"......"

Catching both their gazes, Eiri continued quietly.

"First of all, how about you take this somewhere else? Fighting like this, out in the open—you're bothering everyone around you! Let's clean up the food on the floor and then go somewhere else. You two can take the time to compose yourselves a little—"

"Who asked yoooooooooooooooooooouuuuuuuuuuuuuuuuuuuuu?!"

Ayaka pushed Eiri away with all her strength.

"Kyah?!"

Eiri lost her balance. She fell, pulling over a desk in the process. Textbooks and notebooks scattered everywhere. For several long seconds, her mind stopped. "You're way too strong... You really are Kyousuke's little sister."

"Eiri!" Kyousuke ran over to her. "Are you okay?!"

"…I'm fine," Eiri answered. "I was just a bit startled."

She sat up and glared at her aggressor. "Hey, Ayaka…don't you know the difference between right and wrong?"

Her voice was surprisingly soft.

"That's my line!" Ayaka responded defiantly. "He was taking your side again! Does my big brother really like you that much? He's got terrible taste—you're dumb, you've got a flat chest, and you can't cook. A stinky sow who only gets by on her looks… What is he—"

"Ayaka!" Kyousuke shouted.

"……?!"

Ayaka cowered, looking frightened and bewildered. "B-big brother…?"

Kyousuke could feel guilt stir in his chest as his sister peered up at him with quivering eyes. But letting Ayaka off the hook now wouldn't do her any good, he reminded himself, stoking his anger. "It doesn't matter whose side I'm taking or not taking! I'm angry because you did something cruel."

"……"

"Now apologize."

"…………"

"A single word is fine. Apologize to Eiri, Ayaka."

"………………"

"Hey, how long are you going to stay silent?"

"…………………"

"Apologize!"

Kyousuke shouted again, causing Ayaka's eyes to fill with tears.

Large teardrops fell from her wide eyes.

Steeling himself against the heartache, Kyousuke continued to stare at his sister. She turned her face away, trying to escape his gaze. Wiping her tears, she let out a sob: "B-big brotheeeeeer…"

Kyousuke did not respond.

"Big brotheeeeeeeeerrrr…uuuuuu…"

She sobbed like she was seeking salvation. But Kyousuke did not save her.

Desperately battling the urge to forgive his sister, Kyousuke continued to stare silently at her.

"Uuuuuuuuuuuuuuuuuuuuuuuuuuuuuuuuuuuuuuuu…" Curling into a

ball, Ayaka sobbed and moaned. Her wailing ground away at Kyousuke's heart.

"_____"

Then, the next instant, it abruptly stopped, replaced by the faintest whisper.

"......Wrong."

"Huh?"

"Wrong...wrongwrongwrongwrongwrongwrongwrongwrongwrongwrongwrongwrong wrongwrongwrongwrongwrongwrongwrong wrongwrongwrongwrongwrong, wrong!"

Ayaka shook her head madly, disheveling her hair. Her unfocused eyes seemed to look in different directions.

"Big brother would never say such things... The big brother that Ayaka knows would never be so cruel to her! That's right, he's acting really weird... Ayaka's big brother was always on her side, he protected her, he helped her, he was kind to her, he loved her, but this... this is wrong! Absolutely, completely wrong! This...this isn't the big brother...the big brother that Ayaka knows, this...isn't him..."

"...Huh? What are you saying—"

"Don't touch meeeeeeeeeeeeeeeeeeeeeeeeeeeeeeeeeeeeeeeeeeeeeeeeee!"

Pushing away Kyousuke's extended hand, Ayaka hollered and backed away. After she had put some distance between them, she gazed at him with upturned eyes.

"......Aya...ka?"

The blatant hostility in his little sister's piercing eyes was enough to shake him.

—*Don't touch me.* Ayaka's words stuck in his chest, and he couldn't breathe. His mind went blank.

"......?!"

Kyousuke watched, dumbfounded, as Ayaka turned and ran off wildly.

Wait, please! he tried to cry out, but the words stuck in his throat. In an instant, Ayaka had slipped past Kyousuke's side, crossed before Eiri's eyes, left Maina behind in the classroom, and—

"C'mon, everyone! What are you waiting for, come to the cafeteria— Uwaah?!"

—crashed right into the gas mask that had appeared on the other side of the sliding door, before running off down the hall as fast as her legs could carry her. The sound of her footsteps quickly faded in the distance.

"Owwwwww…what the hell was that? That would have been dangerous if I didn't have my famous boob cushions to protect me! Didn't you learn not to run in the hallway?! Geez…wait, what? Why are you sitting there, Eiri? Your underpants are showing. And what's with the big mess, and all the noise, and…huh? Where's Ayaka?"

Renko, the only one who didn't understand the situation, tilted her head obliviously.

Thirty minutes had passed since the start of the lunch break.

DIE' DIE

IAKA

I'll KILL I'll KILL
YOU YOU

May I Give You Hell?

SELF-QUESTIONING

GUSTINGS

KILL

FADE TO
BLACK

KILL

OU BITCH DIE YOU
DIS

BITCH

U DIRTY DISGUSTING SOW I'll
KILL

The world is nothing but garbage, thought Ayaka Kamiya.

While watching the morning news, while walking through a crowded neighborhood, while listening to a trendy pop song, while having silly conversations with her classmates, while diligently studying, while turning down a friend's invitation, while wearing an approachable smile, she laughed in her mind: *Ah, this is really stupid.*

These feelings had been triggered five years ago—when she was a third-year elementary school student—by malicious, class-wide bullying. The motives behind the bullying were unclear. There may have been no reason to it at all.

Compared to her classmates, Ayaka was prettier, her grades were better, she was more popular with boys, and her teachers liked her best. Her "flawless perfection" might have earned her the ire of her classmates (mainly the girls). Maybe they wanted to revel in the spiteful joy of watching perfect Ayaka stumble and fall.

Just before the bullying had started, Ayaka had turned down a love confession from the most popular boy in her class. The most popular girl in their class liked him. (She was loud and confident and a show-off—the exact opposite of Ayaka. They weren't friends or enemies, though.) —Ayaka thought she'd heard that story, but couldn't remember. She really didn't know who had started it.

She only realized what was going on when her hallway slippers went missing… Afterward, Ayaka became an outcast. Girls who she had thought were her friends threw her gym uniform in the toilet and treated her like a stranger the next day. Girls who she had thought were her best friends gradually stopped spending time with her, and soon ostracized her as well. Afraid of upsetting the other girls, the boys did nothing, and some even supported the bullying, hoping to look favorable to those girls. The teachers pretended to know nothing and to see nothing.

There was no one on Ayaka's side.

Despite all that, at home Ayaka carried on as she always had, wearing a smile on her face. With her whole heart she wished that she would not cause her family too much worry, but at the same time she was living in constant fear. If they knew that Ayaka was being bullied, her papa, and mama, and big brother…it might change how they looked at her, she thought, just like the people at school.

And then one morning about two months after the bullying had started, Kyousuke, who had been in fifth grade then, burst into the third grade classroom. Ayaka had been cleaning graffiti off her desk, in socked feet because she didn't have slippers anymore.

"All of you, look at me!" Kyousuke had shouted. Before the teachers could intervene, he had cornered several of Ayaka's classmates, demanding to know who had made his little sister cry.

After that, the bullying against Ayaka died down. Some people resented Kyousuke and went looking for revenge, but it seemed like he made every one of them cry. The sixth graders were no problem, and even their friends in middle school saw the tables turned when they tried to get their revenge. No one in Ayaka's elementary school could stand up to Kyousuke.

No one wanted anything at all to do with Ayaka or her brother.

…However, Ayaka didn't mind.

In her eyes, her brother was not a violent outlaw; he was her hero and her savior. She became even more emotionally attached to Kyousuke than before, and the two of them began spending more and more time together.

Rumors about Kyousuke had spread even outside of school, and they often ran into trouble, but whenever that happened her big brother always protected her. Time and time again, he was there to rescue her.

That's why she didn't mind it being just the two of them—no, she thought it was for the best, even. Kyousuke's lonely little sister wanted him, and Ayaka's solitary older brother needed her. They were happy like that. *Their world was complete*, and they didn't need anything—or anyone—else.

When she moved to a private middle school, Ayaka attracted a lot of friends, but they were only superficial relationships. They were nothing more than lubricant to make her school life go by smoothly. She didn't get deeply involved with anyone, and no one got deeply involved with her.

They were dirt that she could wash down the drain whenever she wanted. They meant nothing. Almost everything in this world was, after all, disposable—like she had been in elementary school. The people and things she liked were always changing.

There was only one thing that Ayaka could never replace—Kyousuke. Her brother was the one thing Ayaka could never cast aside, no matter what. She would never betray him.

Because he was always on Ayaka's side. He always protected her, and was able to rescue her. He was unerringly kind to her, and forever loved her. Kyousuke was not ordinary garbage. He was a precious treasure.

—In spite of all that...

"Uuu...uuuuuu...uuuuuuuuuuuuuuuuuu!"

In a deserted corner of the school, Ayaka continued sobbing, hugging her knees.

Kyousuke's words and the way he had looked at her before she had escaped the classroom were still stuck in her mind. She couldn't escape them. Her tears fell like blood flowing from a wound.

She felt a deep despair, as if a hole had suddenly opened below her and she was falling into a bottomless darkness. Everything she had cared about, and the world as a whole, was rapidly receding. Ayaka was alone in the depths of an inescapable hell.

"Uuu…why? What did I do, big brother…?"

She thought of Kyousuke now, the Kyousuke she'd met at the academy.

The Kyousuke who, when he looked at Ayaka, was not happy, but started shouting.

The Kyousuke who was surrounded by lots of girls, leading a cheerful school life.

The Kyousuke who brought those other girls along to everything, instead of doing things alone together with Ayaka.

The Kyousuke who never thought about Ayaka's feelings, and only cared about how others felt.

The Kyousuke who snuck around and hid from Ayaka, but flirted with other girls.

The Kyousuke who ate other girls' home cooking, and thought it was okay to call it "tasty."

The Kyousuke who was always scowling and mercilessly shouting at Ayaka.

Each and every one of these was a Kyousuke who Ayaka did not recognize.

Could their time apart have changed her big brother…?

"…No. That's not it. Time didn't change my big brother—"

—*It was them.*

Those murderous girls who hung around Kyousuke. There was no doubt that they had seduced him, deceived him, and driven him mad. There was no doubt that they had damaged Ayaka's precious treasure, tarnished him, polluted him.

That's it. That'sitthat'sitthat'sitthat'sit, that's it!

Ayaka realized that every time Kyousuke got *weird*, those girls had been involved.

Because of Kyousuke's bad reputation, most people kept their distance, and he had no immunity against the charms of the opposite sex. But at this academy people flocked to him, and he was especially popular with the female students. Kyousuke's pure heart had surely been bewildered by the change. Poisoned by those filthy sows, he had lost sight of himself.

He wasn't aware of it, of course, and that was why he had spoken so cruelly to her, and looked at her with such scary eyes. He had been seduced by those girls and only cared about making them happy. That was why he didn't take Ayaka's side.

Of course that's it. I can't imagine anything else.

"......I have to help."

The fear and hopelessness controlling Ayaka melted away, and a sense of purpose welled up in their place. Ayaka had always relied on Kyousuke for help, which was why this time she would help him. It was her turn to rescue her big brother.

But how?

That's obvious, isn't it?

"Tee-hee...tee-hee-hee...tee-hee-hee-hee..."

Her snickering did not stop. She had been feeling the worst, and now she felt the best. When she thought of the things she was going to do—when she thought of Kyousuke, who she was going to save—Ayaka was filled with euphoria so deep she could have drowned in it.

Until now Ayaka had been an ordinary, weak princess, protected by her savior. But from now on it would be different. It wouldn't be like before. If she could save Kyousuke, she too could stand shoulder to shoulder with him. She would become her brother's heroine.

That's why...

"...Wait for me! I'm coming to rescue you. Those disgusting sows won't pollute you any longer, big brother. I promise, I won't let you be defiled!" Ayaka clenched her fists hard in determination. Wiping her tears, she looked boldly ahead.

"Now there's a nice face."

A figure stepped into Ayaka's field of vision. She had no idea how long the person had been standing there. A pair of eyes smiled down on Ayaka, filled with a terribly ferocious, yet somehow gentle, light.

"............Eh?" Ayaka looked confused.

The figure, still smiling, extended a hand toward her. "Why don't I help you make those thoughts of yours a reality?"

Three months ago, that same hand had pulled Ayaka up out of despair and given her hope...

"Yes."

Ayaka took the hand without hesitation.

Q: What is your target rank on the final exams?
Number one. There's no way I can lose to these maniacs!

Q: What are your strongest and weakest subjects?
My strongest subject is...all of them! And I don't have any weak subjects.
Oh, but I guess I don't really "get" ethics...

Q: If you are granted parole, what do you want to do?
I want to flirt with my big brother, just the two of us!
And I don't want anyone getting in the way, so we'll have to do it in my room...
Ee-hee-hee...

Q: Tell us about your enthusiasm for the tests!
Do your best, big brother!
Earn your parole, and we'll lock ourselves away together. ♪

"...Nope. Dammit, she's not anywhere."

"I couldn't find her, either. I went as far as Purgatory Park, but..."

"Ohh, Ayaka...where did you go?"

"It's because the campus is so big. If she's hidden well, it'll be almost impossible to find her."

Classes had ended for the day, and Kyousuke and the others were searching every nook and cranny on the academy grounds. It had been about three hours since Ayaka had run away. She had not returned after lunch break, and was absent during fourth and fifth periods. The punishment for truancy was one concern, but they were most worried about Ayaka's mental state.

Burning impatience and remorse consumed Kyousuke's heart. "It's my fault... Ayaka was shocked because I yelled at her... Shit! If anything happens to her, I'll—"

He struck the door of a nearby janitorial closet in frustration. The steel crumpled loudly, the cacophony echoing through the halls.

A chilly hand covered Kyousuke's trembling fist. "...Calm down. I understand your feelings are running hot, but we've got a job to do, right? Don't lose sight of yourself."

Eiri cast her eyes down, clearly conflicted. Despite her words, she likely felt guilty at giving Ayaka a reason to scold Kyousuke. Her well-chewed lip made that obvious.

"...Oh, you're right. That's right...getting too emotional won't help. Let's calm down. Yeah, just calm down, and focus on finding Ayaka." Unclenching his fists, Kyousuke regained his focus. "Okay. We've finished searching all the usual spots, so that leaves—"

"The new school buildings, maybe? *Kksshh*. But I'm not sure we wanna go there, with how well they treated us last time. I guess if she snuck in while everyone else was in class, she could still be hiding in a toilet stall or something. One place is as good as another, so should we go all together?"

"Let's do that. If push comes to shove, we can ask Miss Shamaya for her help or something..."

Shamaya was supposed to have been disciplined over the lunch break, so it was probably out of the question. Asking her for help right after she had an argument with Ayaka also seemed rather selfish.

"Sweet Shamaya, huh...? *Kksshh*. If it comes to that, just leave it to me! Even if she refuses, I'll force her into submission. I'll show her no mercy!"

"...You really don't go easy on Miss Shamaya, do you?" It was too cruel. Kyousuke couldn't help but feel sorry for her.

Maina spoke up. "Um, um, the other second-year students are taking classes for professional killers, just like Miss Shamaya, right? What if they pick a fight with us...?"

"What, that's no problem! We've got two capable killers right here, don't we?

Me and Eiri...a real odd couple. Have no fear! Giganto Boobs and Tiny Tits are here!"

"That's right. If things get dangerous, Renko can distract them while we escape."

"Eeehhh?! You're cruel, Eiri! Using me as a sacrifice... Who knows what will happen if they catch me? What if the next thing after the Prison School Camping Trip is the School Gang XXXing? It's impossible, my body won't allow it! Though if they try, I'll do my best to buy you some time...oh yeah."

"......Hey, let's get moving...without all the stupid chatter." Fed up with their casual banter, Kyousuke started walking. However, he could feel some of the tension in his frayed nerves ease. Renko had probably said that ridiculous stuff on purpose to get them all to relax.

Eiri lined up with Kyousuke, and Renko and Maina followed behind. Before long, they were in sight of the shoe racks, when—

"......Ah."

A lone student entered the school building behind them. Kyousuke and the others stopped. The skinny girl wore her black hair in pigtails, tied up with purple checkered ribbons. She carried something wrapped in a cloth with both arms.

"......Ah."

When she caught sight of Kyousuke and the others, the girl's eyes grew wide. Looking surprised, she smiled.

"I finally found you!"

Kyousuke and the girl—Ayaka—spoke at the same time. But Ayaka's eyes did not seize upon Kyousuke.

"Tee-hee! I found you...*filthy sows!*"

Instead, Ayaka was staring at Renko and the others. The light was gone from her dark eyes, and her lips were twisted into an expression of wild joy.

Ayaka tore away the cloth wrapping. Faster than anyone could react, she readied the object. About three feet in length, it was—

"Everyone, look out!"

Renko's bloodcurdling scream was immediately followed by an earsplitting boom.

X   X   X

"......Eh?" A small voice broke the silence. Opening her big eyes even wider than ever before, Maina, whose voice was trembling, had fallen over on her backside. "...What...is this?"

A hole had been gouged in the wall behind Maina at almost the exact height that her head had been just a moment before—and Eiri's chest.

Eiri, who had been in front of Maina, stood with her back pressed to the wall. Kyousuke, who had been next to Eiri, was stock-still. Renko, who had been behind Kyousuke, stayed frozen, her hands still pressed against him.

"............"

They all turned slowly to face Ayaka, and were met with an almost unbelievable sight.

A *shotgun*.

A metallic mass of black and brown.

White smoke rose from its upturned barrel.

"Oopsie! Too bad, did I miss? I think my aim's gotten worse." Clutching the gun with both hands, Ayaka stuck out her lip. The cloth she had used to conceal the deadly weapon lay at her feet among spent red shell cases.

"............Huh?"

She'd tried to *shoot* them.

It was hard to believe this was really happening.

Ayaka wore a beaming smile. "Just endure it a little longer, big brother! Ayaka is going to help you now... She's going to exterminate every one of these filthy sows! Ayaka's going to rescue you. Surely that'll turn you back to normal, right? And you'll love Ayaka again?"

"A-Ayaka...what are you saying—?"

"No, it's okay! You're not yourself right now, big brother, so...of course you don't get it. That's why they have to be eliminated first! You can talk with Ayaka after that. She's just going to take them out real quick with the remaining eight rounds, so just hold on! First up is Crafty Cat—"

Ayaka's eyes narrowed as she stared down at Maina, no longer smiling. She carefully balanced the stock of the shotgun atop one shoulder and tried to aim. The way she held the weapon seemed stiff and unnatural.

Yet Maina shrieked and trembled, too afraid to move. "Eek!"

"Tee-hee! How awkward you are, Crafty Cat... You're such a coward. That's a terrible look! But it's okay. Ayaka is going to blow you away in an instant! I'll free you from your fear—along with your heeeeeeeeee-aaaaaaaaad!! You'll be a hole-riddled pulp! Nobody will even be able to recognize you...ah-ha, ah-ha-ha-ha-ha-ha-ha-ah...ah-ha-ha-ha!

Ah-ha-ha-ha-ha-ha-ha-ha-ha-ha-ha-ha!" Ayaka burst into laughter, unable to contain her mad joy as she looked up at the heavens. She had obviously lost her mind.

Maina mumbled, "Ayaka, why…?"

"—Why?" Ayaka's crazy laughter stopped. In a flash, her face grew serious. But her blank eyes reflected no emotion. "You filthy sows—"

Ayaka lowered the shotgun and inhaled deeply.

"Defiled. Big. Brother! That's whyyyyyyyyyyyyyyyyyyyyyyyyyyyyy yyyyyyyyyy!!"

"……?!"

Her hysterical shout caused the air to vibrate. Kyousuke and the others could feel it in their chests.

Ayaka hung her head in sorrow. "You seduced him with your filthy words, and deceived him…you turned him strange. Ayaka's big brother was her treasure…the only one in the world. Her precious, precious treasure. Even so, you all touched him with your filthy hands, and tarnished him…you damaged him. That's why. That's why, see—"

Ayaka lifted her face and smiled again. She giggled, stroking the shotgun.

"—*Ayaka has decided to exterminate you all!* To keep her brother from being defiled any further, you must be eliminated from this world…from *our* world."

Ayaka readied the shotgun once more. Her dark, emotionless eyes seized on their target just as the gun barrel did.

"Eee…," Maina gasped.

Fixing her aim on Maina's forehead, Ayaka slowly squeezed the trigger—

"Wait! Wait, please!"

Another figure, arms spread wide, stood between Maina and the shotgun.

Ayaka frowned. "…Stay out of the way, big brother."

"What are you doing?"

"Eh?"

"What the hell are you doing?" Kyousuke demanded.

Ayaka pouted with a huff and lifted her cheek from the gun. "What do you mean, what? Ayaka told you before! These people are corrupting you, big brother. So, Ayaka is going to eliminate them. Then you won't have to worry about their filth rubbing off on you ever again!"

"I never asked you to do anything like that!"

"……?!" Ayaka visibly withered. "Y-you're still mad…"

Kyousuke took one step toward his newly tearful little sister. "…You said it yourself, didn't you? You said you would never act like this again. You said you didn't want to be a murderer. You said that murder was scary, and you hated it! Are you telling me that was all a lie?!"

"It was not a lie. Ayaka would never lie to you!"

"If that's true, then why—?"

"…Listen, big brother. Ayaka doesn't want to be a murderer. It's scary, and she hates it! But sometimes you have to do something even if you hate it! For Ayaka, this is one of those times. These filthy sows have to die!"

"Filthy sows—you…what kind of grudge do you have against them?!"

"They defiled you, big brother."

"Huh? You said that earlier, too… I'm not defiled."

"Yes! Yes you are."

"…What part of me?"

"*That* part."

"What part?!"

Kyousuke tugged at his hair and ground his teeth in frustration. They were separated by a distance of about thirty feet. Ayaka still had the shotgun readied, so he couldn't move even if he wanted to. He had to try to talk her down, but he just couldn't understand what his beloved little sister was thinking.

Ayaka sighed deeply. "*Haaahhh…* It's no good. *You're not even aware of the symptoms.* You're seriously ill… This is bad. We better hurry up and cut it off at the source. Or else it'll be too late! So, big brother—move!"

"…………"

"Hey, aren't you listening?! Move."

"Ayaka—"

"Listen to Ayaka and move iiiiiiiiiiiiiiiiiiiiiiiiiiiiiiiiiiiiiiiiiiiiiiiiiiiiiiiiiiii iiiiiiiiiiiiiiiiiiiiiiiiiiiiiiiiiiiiiiiiiiiiiiiiiiiiit!"

She fired. The bright flash from the gun muzzle was accompanied by an earsplitting explosion, followed by a scream and the sound of breaking glass.

"Kyah?!"

The shot had missed Eiri by a few inches.

A spent casing and white smoke flew out of the ejection port as the next round was loaded. Recoil had thrown the barrel back, and Ayaka slowly lowered the gun again, head tilted. "...Now. Why won't you listen to what Ayaka says? You are on her side, aren't you, big brother? If so, why are you getting in the way? Why, big brother?"

Ignoring the cracked window, Ayaka took a long, hard look at Kyousuke. Her eyes were entirely devoid of innocence. *She looks just like an insect*, Kyousuke thought. Her jet-black eyes reflected everything and accepted nothing. This creature—with whom he had once felt closer than anyone else—was now completely foreign.

"Uuugh...strange. It's strange! Ayaka is asking you so desperately, so why...why won't you just listen? Can't you understand Ayaka's true feelings? Uuuu...it's true, you really have been defiled. They poisoned your heart and your body, and now you're protecting them...uuuu. Ayaka will not forgive this. She absolutely will not forgive..." Groaning, Ayaka ground her teeth in vexation.

Kyousuke's heart was full of fear, lukewarm and sticky, and he felt a deep sense of loss. He recalled feeling that emotion just for a moment on the day that Ayaka had arrived, and it now gushed rapidly, unstoppable, like blood from a fatal wound.

Overcome by dizziness, Kyousuke shuddered. "What happened to you, Ayaka...?"

Perhaps living in an environment full of murderers had been too stressful for Ayaka to handle. But even without that stress, Ayaka had lost control and tried to commit murder just to see her brother. Even *before* the academy, Ayaka's mind had already been pushed to its limits...

"......No."

An uncomfortable feeling passed over Kyousuke.

Had Ayaka even once mentioned feeling any anxiety toward this strange environment?

Had she showed any fear toward the abnormal students?

—She had not.

Thinking back on it, Ayaka's bouts of selfish violence had always centered on *Renko and the other girls*. This was no different.

It seemed like only Kyousuke, Renko, and the others were reflected in Ayaka's eyes. Renko and the other girls were close to Kyousuke, so—

"……It can't be."

Ayaka wasn't upset by the strange environment or abnormal people. It was only the fact that Kyousuke had gotten so close with members of *the opposite sex* that had left her feeling—

"You're jealous."

"Aaaaaaaaaaaaaaaaaaaaaaaaaaaaaaaaaaaaaaaaaaaaaaaaaaaaaaaaaaaa aaaaaaaaah!"

Ayaka suddenly started shrieking hysterically and shaking her head, making a scene. "It's no use… It's unbearable, this kind of… Ayaka can't stand to look at you like this, big brother! She'll have to do it quickly, quickly…so please move. Move away, big brother!!"

"Wait, Ayaka! I'm begging you, let me explain. I don't know what you're thinking, but these girls are my friends—"

"Shut up! Shutupshutupshutup, shut uuuuuuuuuuuuup! Not another word from my corrupted big brother! That's enough! Move! If you won't move…Ayaka will have to shoot you along with them!!"

"Okay. Go ahead."

"………………………Eh?"

"If I've driven you to the point of killing people, then it's better that I become the victim. But I'm begging you…I'm begging you, please calm down, Ayaka. I couldn't stand it if you became a murderer. Because you're important to me…the most important person in the world!"

"_____"

Ayaka limply lowered the shotgun. "Big brother…" she mumbled with half-closed lips.

Kyousuke smiled in relief. He'd finally gotten through to her.

"……I see." Ayaka smiled again, too. It was not a smile of relief or happiness, but rather a smile of acquiescence. "That's right…you're already so corrupted…okay. You get your way, big brother. Ayaka won't kill these people. Instead—"

Ayaka readied the gun again. The pitch-black muzzle and her pitch-black eyes seized on Kyousuke.

"Ayaka will kill her big brother!"

Ayaka leveled the gun at his forehead. Meeting his gaze, she spoke in a sweet, coaxing voice. "Ayaka will kill you, big brother, and then she'll die, too… If the filthy sows can't be exterminated, then *Ayaka and Kyousuke will have to disappear!* We can be alone together again. No one will get in the way, and no one will defile you. Tee-hee…it's a great idea, isn't it? Don't you think it's the best? Escape from this world, together with Ayaka! In the next world we'll always be together."

"……Aya…ka?"

Ayaka smiled happily at Kyousuke, who stood dumbfounded. "You don't need to be afraid. Ayaka absolutely will not miss… She'll blast your brain stem with one shot, and send you off comfortably. So don't worry! Ayaka will be following right behind you! *See you in heaven, big brother.*"

She pulled the trigger without hesitation.

X   X   X

The gun roared. The shell discharged, without misfiring. The shot did not miss its target. Kyousuke's skull erupted into a spray of fresh blood and brains—or rather, just before it did—

"Kyousuke!"

Eiri reacted immediately and shoved Kyousuke to the ground. Buckshot tore through the air where his head had been just a moment before.

He landed on his back in the corridor. At the same time, Maina, lying helplessly on the floor, shrieked, while Renko roared and leaped forward.

"Waaaaaaaaaaaaahhh!"

She charged at Ayaka, rapidly closing the distance between them.

"Don't get in the waaaaaayyy!"

However, before she had covered even half the distance, Ayaka had finished loading the next round. She aimed at Renko and pulled the trigger.

Again the gun roared.

"Hyah?!"

Renko evaded the shot, rolling forward at an angle. Without losing any momentum, she regained her footing and continued closing in on Ayaka.

The buckshot gouged the linoleum, decorating the hallway with bullet holes.

"...Gah!! Troublesome—aren't you?!"

Though she was clearly surprised by Renko's agility, Ayaka moved quickly. She had already re-aimed the muzzle to point toward Renko, who was still six feet away.

"*Kksshh?!*" Renko, who had been about to leap upon her, had the wind taken out of her sails. She froze in place.

Ayaka's mouth twisted into a broad grin. She fired again, intending to blow off Renko's head.

"......?!"

But the bullet did not fire.

It was *jammed*. Ayaka frantically tried to clear the shell casing jammed in the ejection port.

"*Ffkksshh!*"

"Guh?!"

Renko slammed into Ayaka. She lost her footing and fell.

"...Ah?!"

Ayaka dropped the shotgun.

It slid across the floor: Renko leaped after it immediately, but Ayaka intercepted her.

"As if Ayaka would let yoooooouuuuuu!"

She jumped at Renko from behind, dragging her to the floor.

"Uaaahhh?!"

The two of them rolled down the hall, entangled together. When they finally came to a stop, it was Ayaka who was sitting astride Renko.

"Stay out of Ayaka's waaaaaay, you filthy coooooooooooowww!"

She slapped Renko hard in the face with her right hand.

"Guh... Forget that!" Renko shouted. "I'll get in the way if I want!"

She glared up at Ayaka, then, spitting, "Like hell I'm gonna let you kill

Kyousuke just to satisfy your selfish persecution complex! No matter how much you want to, you'll have to get through me first, little girl!! That is, if you think you can—so how 'bout it?!"

Before Renko had even finished talking, Ayaka hit her with a hard left. She followed up the blow with angry words. "That's just fine, Miss Mask... Ayaka would be glad to butcher you! Since criminals like you all go to hell, you won't end up in the same place as Ayaka and Kyousuke!!"

"What are you talking about? If you kill me, you'll also go to hell! Kyousuke will probably go to heaven, though!! You'll be separated after you die! Too bad, so sad, see you on the other siiiiide!"

"Wha...sh-shut uuup! You're annoooooooooyiiiiiiiing, you filthy piiiiiiiiiiiiiiiiiiiiiiiiiiiiiiiiiig!" Ayaka's face was bright red, and she swung her right fist downward.

Renko pulled away, as if she had been waiting for Ayaka's attack, and evaded the blow.

"Ah—"

Ayaka struck the floor just as Renko's fist slammed into her cheek.

"...Bwuh?!"

Ayaka recoiled.

Renko was up in an instant.

"The only pig here is yooooooooouuuuuuu!!"

Tossing Ayaka aside, she quickly reversed their positions. This time, Renko was on top.

Renko grabbed Ayaka by the collar with one hand and peered down into her face. "You don't get to go around killing people just because things don't go your way! How conceited can you be?! You should only be selfish when it comes to your body! That's impossible for someone with a skinny body like you, though! If I'm a pig, you're a chicken carcass, huuuh?!"

"Bwuu?!"

She slapped Ayaka on the left cheek.

Ayaka's eyes welled up with tears, and she glared hatefully. "...You ...you shut up! Don't get such a swollen head! Not after defiling my brother! The only things on you that should be swollen are your boobs, milk cow! Holstein!"

"Yeah, yeah, you're just jealous! They're perfectly fiiiiiiiirm! And anyway, it's too bad for you, because Kyousuke loves big boobs! Looks like you don't know anything about him, do yoooooouuu?!"

"You're the one who doesn't know anything! He doesn't go for enormous breasts, he likes well-shaped ones, so theeeeeere!! Will you stop talking like you know everything?! You can't just go around acting like that, you knoooooow!"

Ayaka grabbed Renko's boobs with both hands and hit her with a surprise head-butt.

"*Kksshh?!*"

Shoving the stunned young woman away, Ayaka took a mount position. She slapped the gas mask over and over again. "Ayaka understands him! Ayaka understands perfectly well! Better than anyone else, Ayaka knows her big brotheeeeeer! There's no way she can lose to someone like you...to some *newcomer* who only just met him! She can't lose, no waaayyy! Die! Diediediedie, diiiiiiiiiiiieeeeeeeeee!"

Despite being jolted to the right and left by Ayaka's blows, Renko turned back to her each time. Focusing on Ayaka's face, she raised her voice. "You *understand*?! Do you really—buh!! Do you really understand?! I don't think so! If Kyousuke—buh!! If you understood Kyousuke, this act—buh!! This whole charade, where you act like a killer in front of your brother—you wouldn't be able to do it! —Buh!! I won't lose! To a girl like you—buh!! As if I would let a self-righteous, blindly devoted, *fanatic* with terrible judgment like you take me ooooooouuut—buh!!"

Ayaka grew angrier and angrier, but Renko would not shut her mouth at all, no matter how many times she was hit. Ayaka struck her with the palms of her hands, alternating left and right, her pigtails fraying.

"Shut up! Shutupshutupshutupshutup, shut uuuuuuuuuup!"

"Now who needs to shut up?! Nyeh-nyeh-nyeh! Your shrill voice is hurting my ears!"

"Quiet, witch!"

"You be quiet, bitch!"

"You're one to talk!"

"So are you! I'm way better-looking!!"

"...Oh, please! You always have a comeback, you filthy sow—"

"That's Ayaka's liiiiiiiiiiiine!"

Renko threw herself at Ayaka, who was getting short of breath from all the slapping, trying to reverse their positions again. Ayaka resisted, undaunted, and the two of them rolled farther down the hall, still entangled.

Drawn by the commotion, curious students began to gather one by one to watch.

"Wha?! Whaddaya know, if it ain't a catfight! Kill her, kill her!"

"Hee-hee-hee…flushed, entangled bodies…disheveled clothes and ragged breathing…hee-hee…"

"Renko?! And…Ayaka, isn't it? What are you two doing?!"

"…I think it's cannibalism. In this world it's survival of the fittest, after all. The loser will be devoured by the winner."

"Hee-hee-hee, you're completely right, Chihiro… Strength is everything! Power is absolute! Only the true strongest person can reign as Absolute Emperor—waaaaaahhh?! A shotgun! There's a shotgun lying over there!! No way!! Hey, is that gun real?!"

On the right and left sides of the hallway, and in the entrance hall, students surrounded them on three sides.

No one tried to force their way between the two girls.

They watched intently as Renko and Ayaka fought, ignoring their audience.

"_____"

Kyousuke and the others were no exception. They had not even moved. Eiri was still on top of Kyousuke, Kyousuke was still under Eiri, and Maina was still cowering, frozen in fear, as they all watched the two combatants struggle.

Renko and Ayaka smashed against each other with their bodies and words, each of them fighting furiously for the upper hand. No third party could have easily intervened.

Their argument filled the entryway, now overflowing with students.

"*Kksshh!* How about thinking of Kyousuke's feelings for once, Ayaka?!"

"Ayaka is always thinking about them! More than someone like you—all the time!"

The two of them had gotten to their feet and were facing off, pulling each other's hair.

"No, you don't! You just selfishly force your ideals on him, don't you?!"

"Ayaka doesn't force anything! Her big brother accepts her!"

"You couldn't get him to accept you, could you?! But escaping from reality is your specialty, right?!"

"Only because you all defiled hiiiiiiiiimmm!!"

"See, there's that escapism! That's enough, nutcase!"

"Yeah, enough from you, bitch!"

"What was that?!"

"What did you say?!"

They strained and butted heads, glaring at each other. They both looked like a mess, with disheveled hair and wrinkled clothing. Ayaka's face was covered in fresh bruises and cuts, and Renko's gas mask looked like it might come loose at any moment.

.........Huh?

Her gas mask is about to come off?

Without the gas mask—her limiter—Renko was like a wild animal without a muzzle. As the Murder Maid, created only to kill, she was entirely capable of slaughtering anyone she laid eyes upon. She was usually locked into her mask by a fixed band, but...

In life-threatening situations, Renko's unlimiter would kick in and release the lock. The fistfight with Ayaka could have caused that mechanism to go into operation, though it didn't look to Kyousuke like she'd been driven to that point yet.

Still, he was sure that thing was about to dislodge, and it would be bad news time then.

"Hey, stop it!" Climbing to his feet, Kyousuke pushed Eiri out of the way and tried to rush over to the two of them. "Renko, Ayaka! Don't fight any more!"

"This...is...annoyiiiiiiiiiiiiiiiiiiiiiing!"

Ayaka screamed as her flying knee kick struck Renko's stomach.

"*Kksshhggh?!*" Renko staggered and released her hold on Ayaka's hair.

"Diiiiiiiiiiiiiiiiiiiiiiiiiiiiiiiiiiiiiiiiiiiiiiiiiiiiiiiiiiiiiieeeeeeeeeeeeeeeeeeeeeeeeeeeeeeeeeeeee!"

Ayaka landed a right straight punch on Renko's face with all her might.

"Gyah?!"

Renko was sent sprawling by the blow. She staggered back a sizable distance. From her face, which had been turned away from Kyousuke by Ayaka's punch, something fell.

"......?!"

The spectators looked on breathlessly.

Renko did not make the slightest movement.

At her feet lay the jet-black gas mask.

"_____"

The tumult of the crowd went still, their enthusiasm cooled in an instant. A strange air of tension enveloped the area.

"............Ah."

A confused voice.

Renko turned back to face Ayaka, who was still frozen in the follow-through to her punch.

"...Hee-hee-hee."

The mask had fallen away, revealing her bare face.

Her peach-colored lips were twisted into a smile.

"That was a serious punch, huh...? Hee-hee-hee! It even knocked my mask right off! Aaah...what shall I do with you, Ayaka dear? *It's started playing...!* A violent melody, the likes of which I've never heard before! Ooohhh!"

"......?!"

Renko's transparent, ice-blue eyes were reminiscent of a glacier at absolute zero.

Staring at her terribly beautiful face, Ayaka was frozen solid. Her eyes were wide with shock, and she opened and closed her mouth as if trying to speak.

The students surrounding them looked the same. Overwhelmed by Renko's bare face—by her beauty—they seemed to have lost their voices.

In the silence, a clear soprano rang out.

"Huh? Hey, hey, hee-hee-hee...everyone, you all look like you've been bewitched by my exceptional beauty. Oh noooooo, it really is a sin to be too beautiful! I haven't even done anything yet, and I've already killed everyone's hearts en masse! Tee-hee! Hee-hee...well, then. How about I destroy your bodies next? Body and soul, completely—"

"Ah...uu...uu, uaaaaaaaaaaaaaaaaaaaaaaaaaaaaaaaaaaaaaaaaaaaahh hhhhhhhhhhhhhh!"

Ayaka screamed. Turning her back on Renko, she dashed toward the exit.

"Ah?! Wait a minute, little Ayaka! Don't run away!"

—But Ayaka was not fleeing.

Quite the opposite. She was not headed for the exit, but for something nearby. The shotgun, which had been forgotten during the scuffle, still lay where it had fallen behind a shoe rack. Ayaka snatched up the gun, pointed it at Renko, and squeezed the trigger.

Renko flinched. "Wah?!"

A thunderous roar rang out.

The crowd shrieked.

But the shot missed the mark. It carved a hole in the bulletin board behind Renko.

Renko stuck both hands out in front of her. "Stop! Ayaka, stoooooop!"

Of course, there was no way Ayaka could stop.

"Eeeeeek?! Look out, look out! Eeeaaahhh!!"

She rapid-fired one, two, three rounds. One thunderous roar after another, after another.

However, none of them hit.

Renko wasn't dodging the shots. Ayaka's aim was off. She seemed uncharacteristically shaken by Renko's aura.

After the third shot, Ayaka bellowed as if giving way to despair.

"Aaaaaaaaaaaaaaaaaaaaaaaaaaaaaaaaaaaaaaaaaaaaaaaaaaaagggggghhh hhhh!"

Readying the shotgun again, she thrust it straight forward.

The distance between the two girls closed in a flash.

"_____"

Renko stared Ayaka down with narrowed ice-blue eyes.

Ayaka pointed the barrel of the gun at Renko's face and gritted her teeth.

Renko coiled into a low crouch.

And then—

☓   ☓   ☓

A taut silence descended.

Everyone held their breath and stared at the spectacle before their eyes.

"……What's wrong, Ayaka?" Renko asked, smiling. Sharp, white canine teeth peeked out from between her plump lips. "If you're going to kill me, you'd better do it soon."

She pressed the muzzle of the gun to her forehead.

The barrel trembled slightly. Her ragged breathing was audible.

"Fuu, fuu…fuuuuuu!"

Ayaka gritted her teeth and steadied the shotgun with both hands. Her bloodshot eyes were wide-open. With her index finger still on the trigger, she defiantly met Renko's icy gaze.

But Renko appeared unconcerned. She shrugged indifferently. "Go on, squeeze the trigger! Just like the last eight shots. It's easy! Even I would be helpless if you shot me from this range. There's no way you can miss."

"……Kill you."

"Yeah. If I'm such a hateful nuisance, you'd better kill me."

"……Kill! Killkillkillkillkillkillkill, kill!"

"Umm, yeah. But you can't do it just by moving your mouth. Don't you want to kill me?"

"Sh-shut up! Be quieeeeeeeeet! You'll get your wish! I don't need you to tell me what to do."

"Stop it!" Kyousuke shouted. He fell to his knees. "Please stop, Ayaka… Don't kill Renko…I'm begging you."

"Big brother—" Ayaka looked on him with a half-lidded stare. As before, her dark eyes did not harbor even the faintest light. "Hmm… so she *is* important to you?"

"She's important. Of course she is."

"Oh, that's right…you've been poisoned, haven't you? But it's all right. Because Ayaka is going to kill Miss Mask. And once she's dead,

Ayaka will kill you, too, big brother, and then herself...tee-hee! Right, well, we'd better get started." She began to turn back to face Renko. "This time, right between the eyes—"

"I meant that Ayaka is important!" Kyousuke shouted, baring his true feelings. "You are important to me, so I don't want you to kill anyone! Especially not one of my friends... You may be jealous of Renko and the other girls, but you are an irreplaceable member of my family! You're the one and only! Seeing you like this... If you commit murder over something like jealousy, I would...I would—"

"Hey, Ayaka..." Renko asked, in a quiet soprano voice. She gazed at Ayaka's face. "You think nothing of doing that, do you?"

Ayaka furrowed her brow in suspicion and glared at her opponent. "What was that? If you're talking about killing you, then not reall—"

"Not that. I'm talking about Kyousuke. He looks like he's in awful agony, doesn't he...? He looks sad, and in pain, doesn't he? Don't you care that you made someone so important to you look like that? I'm asking you, Ayaka."

"Hmm......" Ayaka seemed to falter, just for a moment, but her eyes quickly filled with anger. "You're the ones who have been hurting big brother! You all corrupted him... All of this is your fault!! If only you all weren't here, Ayaka wouldn't need to do things like this! Ayaka never made her big brother look like that... It's all your faaaaaauuuuuuult!"

When she had finished squealing, Ayaka stood panting hard. *"Fuu, fuu!"*

Renko calmly waited for Ayaka to catch her breath before answering. "—For your information, little Ayaka..." Her lips curved into a ferocious smile, showing off fangs that glittered like knives. *"I can kill you at any time!* I could break your arms faster than you could pull that trigger, and I could blow off your head faster than that gun could fire...hee-hee! A few seconds would be plenty of time to deal with a fragile little human like you. I wouldn't even need a weapon. It wouldn't be necessary. I could tear you to shreds with my bare hands and scatter the pieces!"

Renko stuck her tongue out. Her eyes blazed, and her pupils were dilated.

"...Uh." Ayaka cowered in awe.

"But *I'm not going to kill you*. Do you understand why that is?"

"I…I don't know, I don't get you! Anyway, I don't really—"

"Because Kyousuke would be sad."

Renko's expression seemed almost gentle. Possibly, when she had been watching Kyousuke eat Ayaka's cooking during cooking class, Renko might have been wearing such an expression underneath her mask.

"……?!"

Ayaka's eyes were wide.

Renko held her gaze as she continued. "I love Kyousuke. I can't bear the thought of making him sad. So for the sake of my love, Kyousuke, I can kill even the strongest murderous impulses. I can kill jealousy. I can kill uneasiness. I can kill selfishness. I can kill my own raison d'être. I can kill my own identity. And even if I can't kill it, I'll still try!"

"Wha…?"

Ayaka was speechless. Renko's words had been as plain and direct as her stare.

The formidable young woman narrowed her ice-blue eyes. "And what about you, Ayaka? For Kyousuke's sake, can't you kill your own feelings? Are your feelings for Kyousuke that strong?"

"…Sh-shut up."

"In the end, you are your own most important person, aren't you, Ayaka? Not Kyousuke! You make up excuses, about how he was 'poisoned' and 'defiled,' but you really only care about your own feelings, don't you?!"

"…Shut up."

"Good grief. I'm very disappointed, Ayaka. It turns out that the most important person in the world to you isn't Kyousuke at all…it's you! What an easy victory! Heh-heh-heh! You can't even kill your own murderous impulses… How could you ever think you could kill me? Come now, what's wrong? If you think you can do it, then do it!! Ah-ha-ha!"

"Shut uuuuuuuuuuuuuuuuuuuuuuuuuuuuuuuuuuuuuuuuup!"

Howling hysterically, Ayaka readied the gun again.

Her bloodshot eyes were open as wide as they would go.

The barrel trembled against Renko's forehead.

"I'll kill you… I'llkillyouI'llkillyouI'llkillyouI'llkillyouI'llkillyou

I'llkillyouI'llkillyouI'llkillyouI'llkillyouI'llkillyouI'llkillyouI'llkillyou
I'llkillyouI'llkillyouI'llkillyouI'llkillyouI'llkillyouI'llkillyouI'llkill
youI'llkillyouI'llkillyouI'llkillyouI'llkillyouI'llkillyouI'llkill
youI'llkillyouI'llkillyou, I'll kill you…!"

Ayaka was muttering to herself like she was reciting an incantation. Renko stared down at her tear-filled glare.

"Ayaka!

"Ayaka dear!"

"……Uu…uuuu…uuuuuuuuu!"

As Kyousuke, Maina, and Eiri watched attentively, Ayaka groaned and gritted her teeth. They weren't sure whether she was trying to pull the trigger or trying to prevent herself from doing so.

"Uu…uuu…"

Before long, Ayaka's face crumpled and distorted, and tears ran down her cheeks.

The shotgun fell from her weakened grasp.

"Uaaaaaaaaaaaaaaaaaaaaaaahhh!"

Ayaka broke down crying, and covered her face with both hands, sobbing as the words spilled from her mouth. "I love my big brother… I love him more than someone like Miss Mask ever could. I love him so muuuch! I love him, I love him, and I don't want to give him up to anyone else…because my big brother is my greatest treasure…because he's the only one in the world, the only family I can count on!"

Ayaka continued sobbing as she poured out her feelings to Kyousuke.

"I didn't want you to be taken away by Miss Mask and Miss Akabone-head and Crafty Cat… I really, really didn't want them to steal you away! If my big brother went away, I'd be so lonely again… It would be too awful! I couldn't stand it. I've only got you, big brother… uuuuuuaaa… Don't leave me, big brotheeeeeeeeerrr…!"

"A-Ayaka—"

"It's okay, Ayaka dear."

Before Kyousuke could rush over, Renko knelt down beside her. "There, there…" She placed a hand on Ayaka's head and gently stroked her hair. "You love Kyousuke, and Kyousuke loves you. You love each other as brother and sister. Is that relationship something that can be broken easily? Is it a fragile bond that will suddenly snap apart if other people try to split you up, Ayaka?"

"No! It's not like that!!" Ayaka quickly raised her head with a glower.

Renko nodded with satisfaction. "Right!" She smiled broadly. "And if that's true, you don't need to worry, do you? Besides, I don't want to steal Kyousuke from you. I just want to let me be a part of your world."

"......Uh."

"Of course, I don't mean right away! We've still only just met, and I'm going to work hard to win your trust! I like you. Honestly, at first I thought I had to get close to you because you were Kyousuke's little sister, but...can I get along with a girl who likes the same boy as me, I wondered? Then I realized that I had to set that aside and try to become good friends with you, Ayaka."

"_____"

Ayaka cast her eyes down again.

She chewed on her lip.

"Uh, ummm...of course that won't work, huh? You don't want to be friends with a murderer like me! Actually, right now at this very moment, I can't help but want to kill you... I won't kill you now, because Kyousuke would be sad, but eventually I'll kill Kyousuke... and you along with him..."

"......nothing to do."

"Hm?"

"It has nothing to do with you being a murderer! Ninety-nine percent of this world is worthless garbage...so people like that aren't worth worrying about. I don't care about them, no matter what. If they get in the way, I should erase them. I think nothing of it. I don't have any feelings of ill will, or guilt about getting rid of garbage. Not at all...none."

"...Is that so?"

"But..."

Her gaze faltered. Ayaka looked almost bewildered.

"—I didn't shoot you."

She looked down at her right hand, at her finger resting on the trigger. "I couldn't kill Miss Mask... Miss Mask would die. 'She'll disappear'—when I thought that, suddenly my chest started to hurt.

I remembered all kinds of things, like going around the school buildings together, and running away from the upperclassmen, and the study party, and cooking class..."

"Ayaka..."

"I was really angry at you. Why couldn't I kill you? What was so difficult about cleaning up one piece of garbage...? But now I think I understand."

Ayaka looked hard at Renko with upturned eyes, blushing faintly. "The reason I couldn't kill you...it wasn't because my big brother would hate it. I couldn't kill you because *I* would hate it. Miss Mask, you're—

"*Miss Renko*, you've already become so much more than ordinary garbage."

"_____"

Renko was silent.

"Ah, um...Miss Renko?"

Ayaka knit her eyebrows, looking concerned.

"Uu...uuaaaaaaaaaaaaaaaaaaaaaaaaaaaaaaaaaaaaaaaaaaaaaaaaaaaaaaa aaahhh!!"

Renko fell to the floor, rolling back and forth and screaming like she had gone mad.

"Hyah?! What's wrong, Renko—?"

"Don't come any closer!"

As Ayaka was about to approach her, Renko shouted and slammed her head into the floor. "Ah, this is bad... This melody is bad neeeeeews! An ultra-high-speed sweep, then a gravity blast, and a torrent of seven-string bass kicks in like a drill—aaaaaah, it's intense! It's too inteeeense!! I-I want to kill...I wanttokillwanttokillwanttokillwanttokillwanttokillwanttokill wanttokillwanttokillwanttokillwanttokillwanttokillwanttokillwantto killwanttokillwanttokill, I want to kiiiiiill! What amazing techno-death! I can't control it... This violent melody, it's out of controoooooooool!!"

"Renko?! Wait! Right now, your gas mask—"

Kyousuke picked up the limiter and hurried over to where Renko was writhing in pain. Ayaka and the other astonished onlookers watched, without really understanding what was going on, as he replaced it on her head.

X   X   X

"...I'm disappointed in you, Miss Kamiya."

Kurumiya had brought Kyousuke and the others to the staff room in the new school after Ayaka's shooting incident. She sat with her legs stretched out on the black office desk and blew purple smoke in Ayaka's face. The five of them stood lined up, side by side, before her.

Ayaka coughed, and then looked at Kurumiya with upturned eyes. "You're disappointed, Miss Kurumiya...but you gave me the gun, didn't you?"

"Indeed," Kurumiya readily admitted.

"Not 'indeed'!" Ayaka shouted.

Nobody was entirely surprised to learn that Kurumiya was the one who had lent Ayaka the shotgun. Apparently, Kyousuke and the others had not been able to find Ayaka during their search of the school because Kurumiya had hidden her. While they were in class, Ayaka had been learning how to handle a gun from a teacher named Mizuchi on the *shooting range* in the new school building.

Kurumiya, who had masterminded the whole affair, shrugged her shoulders. "I'm not upset that you caused a disturbance. But just like the first time, you didn't kill a single person—that's why I'm disappointed, you idiot! You fired off eight rounds and missed with every single one of them! It's one thing to get a failing grade, but you failed the makeup test, too! Don't joke around."

"You're the one who must be joking!!"

Kyousuke leaned forward in excitement and grabbed Kurumiya by the collar. "What did you make my little sister do, you sadistic old hag? I'll slaughter you, bitch!!"

Kurumiya looked downright joyful. "Ohh, so you finally feel like killing! Very well, Kamiya. From now on I'll be sure to pay little Miss Kamiya plenty of special attention. If your little sister suffers terribly, maybe then you'll show me what you can do! Hee-hee-hee...! Just like I thought, letting your sister transfer here was the right call."

"Wha—?! Y-you—"

Kurumiya's words had cooled Kyousuke's anger just as it had been about to boil over. *Letting her transfer, she said. Could that mean that she approved the transfer, regardless of Ayaka's "attempted" murder? Or possibly…?*

"Before she came to the academy, someone gave Ayaka a shotgun. Was it you, Kurumiya?"

"It was not."

"Huh? Then who on earth—?"

"Obviously, it was the delivery driver. I'm the one who sent it, but I'm not the one who gave it to her. Why would you think that I would go out of my way to deliver it in person?"

"You're splitting hairs!"

"Shut up."

Kurumiya ground her cigarette into Kyousuke's forehead.

"Ah! Hot!"

Kyousuke let go of Kurumiya.

She stared at him boldly. "…Why are you so upset? Shouldn't you be grateful? Thanks to the fact that the gun I gave her misfired, little Miss Kamiya didn't actually kill anyone after all."

"Ah?! You're full of shit! If you hadn't sent a gun to Ayaka—"

"Sooner or later, Miss Kamiya probably *would* have *killed* someone."

"……Huh?"

"I merely hurried her along. If she didn't have a gun, it would have been a knife, and if she didn't have a knife, it would have been a blunt weapon, and if she didn't have a blunt weapon, it would have been her bare hands… I'm sure she would have killed someone. In order to follow you, understand? This time was no different. Even if I hadn't gone out of my way to get involved, Miss Kamiya would probably have tried to eliminate Renko and the other girls. —Right, Miss Kamiya?"

"…………"

Ayaka did not answer Kurumiya's question. She remained silent, and neither affirmed nor denied the accusation. Her sulky, averted eyes told them exactly what was on her mind.

"She's still a virgin—barely—but it's clear that Miss Kamiya is a psychopath. She thinks nothing of murder, after all. Without you, her limiter, around, she could easily step over the line. And anyway, the person who warped Miss Kamiya's sense of right and wrong was… you, Kamiya."

…He couldn't refute that.

Kyousuke himself was beginning to understand it a little. The way that he had rescued Ayaka from bullying before had been too forceful, and that had narrowed Ayaka's world. Limited relationships had given rise to abnormal attachments, and his excessive affections had warped Ayaka's sense of right and wrong. Every time he'd raised a hand to protect Ayaka, he'd only pushed her further down into darkness...

That was why Kyousuke could not blame his sister. He'd driven her to violence in the first place, and he should be the one to accept the blame—

"No. My big brother didn't do anything wrong."

Ayaka's tone was forceful. She placed a hand on her chest and closed her eyes, speaking wistfully. "My big brother saved me. Not just this time...but time and time and time and time again he always helped me, and he always protected me. If my big brother hadn't been there, I probably wouldn't be here now. So I don't want him to blame himself. Don't apologize, big brother! Don't think that saving me was a mistake... I'm the one who was wrong. I depended on you too much. I'm sorry, big brother."

"Ayaka..."

"...Tch." Kurumiya clicked her tongue and flopped down in her chair. "Ahh, this is boring. Boring, boring, really boring! Leave the soap opera out of it. I'm done with you two—get lost already! I'll overlook it this time."

"...If anything's being overlooked, it's your actions."

"Shut up, Akabonehead."

"...You first." Cursing under her breath, Eiri left the staff room.

"Oh dear..." Maina followed after her.

Kyousuke and Ayaka also moved toward the exit, when Kurumiya spoke up.

"Oh, and, Kamiya...regarding the conditions of your graduation—*let's include your sister, too.* If Miss Kamiya makes it to her graduation ceremony alive and without killing anyone, I will let her graduate into the free world. By the way, I've already told her about the true nature of this academy, so there no need for you to explain."

"...Thanks for that. I was going to ask you."

"Yep! If it's for my big brother's sake, I'll do my best, too!"

"Hee-hee-hee! Struggle as hard as you can, Kamiya siblings. And then there's Murder Maid—" Her smile disappeared, and Kurumiya turned her half-closed eyes on Renko. She glared at the gas mask for a moment. "…No, it's fine. You get lost, too."

"*Kksshh-shh-shh!*" Renko just laughed, and turned on her heel without saying a word.

Kyousuke took Ayaka's hand and they headed finally for the door. As they were leaving, they caught sight of Kurumiya, face twisted with anger, fiddling with her cell phone.

"—Kill 'em."

"I'm disappointed in Miss Kurumiya!" The moment they left the staff room, Ayaka exploded with anger. "To think she was such a mean person... It's just like you said, big brother! Miss Kurumiya is not a good teacher. She's a bad teacher who was going to trick us and try to turn us into professional killers! She's rotten by nature, that little pip-squeak."

"H-hey...'pip-squeak' is a taboo word. Don't ever say it. If she heard you—"

"Pip-squeak! Pip-squeak, pip-squeak, stupid pip-squeak! Miss Kurumiya the pip-squeeeaaak!"

"Quit it!" Clapping a hand over Ayaka's mouth, Kyousuke pulled her away from the staff room.

"But she is tiny and annoying, isn't she?"

"She is, but don't be reckless." Kyousuke scratched the back of his head and sighed. "If you keep antagonizing her like that, it'll blow up in your face! It's like when thugs and criminals would zero in on me because when I went on a rampage, I didn't care who I ended up fighting."

"...Hmph. Well, I always choose carefully."

"Really?"

"Yeah."

"But you were wrong about Kurumiya, weren't you?" Kyousuke insisted.

"I-it happens..."

"And going the other way...you turned on Renko, and she ended up being a good person, didn't she?"

Ayaka kept silent, and Kyousuke continued: "Don't you think you ought to decide if someone is your enemy after you get to know them, instead of attacking them right away? You might throw something away, thinking it's garbage, and it could turn out to be treasure, right? If so, I think it's a terrible waste."

"......" Hanging her head, Ayaka made a tight fist. She bit her lip. "Miss Akabonehead! Crafty Cat!" she called out in a loud voice.

Eiri and Maina turned back to look at Ayaka.

"…What?"

"Wh-what is it…?"

Eiri leaned against the wall, scowling, and Maina answered timidly.

Ayaka lifted her face and met their gazes. "I'm sorry!" she said, and bowed her head. "I'm sorry for saying and doing lots of cruel things. Even if Miss Akabonehead aggravated me and was getting unreasonably physical, I said too much. And even if Crafty Cat was cunning and irritating, I went too far. I regret it. I'm sorry!"

"Ummm, was that…supposed to be an apology?"

"M-maybe… I think so."

Ignoring their confused looks, Ayaka continued. "…I realize it now. The reason I felt so uneasy was because I didn't trust the people I was with. But I trust my big brother! So I've decided to stop being worried that someone will 'steal' him. And—"

Ayaka looked up at Eiri and Maina.

"I'm going to try to trust the people that my big brother believes in. So, ummm…*Miss Akabane, Miss Igarashi!* Would you please…be my friends?"

"_____"

Silence descended on the group.

Eventually, Eiri sighed. "…Whatever, fine. But don't call me Miss Akabane!"

"Eh. H-huh…? Akabane—Miss Akabonehead, you're not mad?"

"I'm not mad. I'm used to it. I'm used to dealing with my own little sister, and I'm also used to suffering through other unpleasant experiences. Just—"

Her head still turned away, Eiri glanced over with half-lidded eyes.

"Don't call me 'Miss Akabonehead,' either, would you? It's better than using my family name, but it's still irritating… Eiri is fine. Get my name right, and I guess I can forgive you."

"Uh, ummm…Miss E-Eiri?"

"Yeah." Eiri smiled gently. "That's fine."

Taking a long, hard look at her, Ayaka repeated, "…Miss Eiri." She did not sound entirely sure of herself.

"Um! I also want to be friends with you, Ayaka," Maina said. "You were awfully scary when you tried to kill us…but I've been in the same situation. If you'll accept someone as stupid and dangerous as me, I'd like to get to be your fwend! Oh…I messed it up…"

"Miss Igarashi…you are doing that on purpose, right?"

"Ehhh?! It-it wasn't on purpose, I'm telling you!"

"Hmm, you didn't fumble it this time…very suspicious. As I thought, Crafty Cat is still crafty. My suspicions about you might be right after all."

"Eeehh, th-that's…oh no…"

"Don't worry about it, Crafty Cat." Eiri grinned.

"You too, Eiri?!"

"Tee-hee!" Ayaka laughed at the development.

"*Kksshh!*" Renko laughed, too, watching the exchange. "Looks like you've reconciled one way or another, huh? Yep, yep…and they all lived happily ever after! By the way, Ayaka, about me—?"

"…Hmm?"

Ayaka listened with a serious expression as Renko told her story. She talked about how she was a professional killer who had been created as a tool for murder; about how her kill count was in the hundreds; about how every single one of her emotions urged her to *kill*; about how her gas mask was a limiter that restrained her irresistible murderous impulses. She told Ayaka about how right now that impulse was contained by unrequited love, and how once it became mutual love, she would feel the need to kill even Kyousuke…

"_____"

When she had finished listening to Renko's story, Ayaka hung her head, and shut her mouth tight. Her bangs cast a shadow over her face, obscuring her expression.

"Aah…s-sorry! My true nature is supposed to be a secret, so I couldn't tell you until now. Um, what can I say, just…I'm sorry. I love Kyousuke, so I want him to change his mind about me, but if he does, I'll probably kill him, so…ummm…s-sorry! I'm not trying to steal Kyousuke away from you! When I kill Kyousuke, I'll kill you along with him! If I do that, you can be together in the next life, like you said, right?! A-and everyone lived happily ever after…"

"No they didn't," Kyousuke spat.

Renko ignored the jab. As she fidgeted awkwardly, searching for the right words to explain, Ayaka slowly lifted her face.

"*Endure it, please.*"

She spoke bluntly, wearing a wide smile.

"Miss Renko, you said it yourself, didn't you? You said, 'for the sake of my love Kyousuke, I can kill even the strongest murderous impulse.' If that's true, please kill it properly even after it becomes mutual love. Don't kill my big brother, kill your own killer desires."

"Ehh?! I mean, I did say that, but…the stronger my feelings become, the stronger my deadly desires get! If I didn't have my mask, it would always be resounding through my head!!"

"I don't know. What, are you giving up…? Can't you kill your own murderous impulses, even for my big brother's sake? Are your feelings that strong?"

"*Kksshh?!* Th-that's…"

"Oh, I see. In the end, you are your own most important person, aren't you, Renko? You offer excuses, but you really only care about your own feelings, don't you? Tee-hee!"

"You're wrong! Kyousuke is more important to me that anything, more precious than anyone…"

"Of course." Ayaka smiled. "And if that's true, then you will endure it, won't you?!"

"_____"

Is this her idea of revenge?

Renko was clearly at a loss. "Uuu…th-that's r-right. If I really love Kyousuke, I have to endure. It's as you say, Ayaka…ohh… Wh-what's this…if it becomes mutual love like this, I won't be the least bit satisfied, will I? —Ah!! But, but! If Kyousuke ever *wants* me to kill him, you won't mind if I do it, will you?!"

"Alright, fine. If that's what my big brother wants, it's all right!"

"…Is it?" Kyousuke asked.

"Sure! But when it's time, you have to kill me along with him, okay? I don't want to be separated from my big brother. As long as Miss Renko is the one killing me, it's okay…yay! Eee-hee-hee…"

"Is it…?" Kyousuke repeated. He felt slightly dizzy looking at his little sister's bright smile.

"*Kksshh!*" Renko looked overjoyed, and embraced Ayaka tightly. "Ayaka! I'll do my best… I'll try hard! To make Kyousuke fall in love with me, and to endure my murderous impulses…I'll try to make him fall so deeply in love that he wants to give his life to me!"

"Sure. If that's how you feel, there's no helping it, so…I approve of your approach. I learned all kinds of things from you, Miss Renko… so this is your repayment! B-but it doesn't really mean that I like you, or that I'm accepting you, okay?!"

Kyousuke looked back and forth between the two of them with very mixed feelings. *Frankly, there's still one huge problem…* The thought of killing someone did not seem to bother Ayaka much. Apparently her underlying way of thinking and sense of values hadn't changed at all. Kurumiya was right—there was a danger that she might kill if something set her off.

"Ayaka baaaby!"

"Oww!! Your gas mask keeps hitting me! And if you're going to hit me, only use your boobs! Speaking of which, how about taking it off already? It's a nuisance for you to always be wearing that thing. It's a waste. Look, it'll probably make my big brother happy, too!"

"Ah, yeah. You're right, for sure! Why don't I take it off? I've also been thinking I'd be better off without it. This time of year, it gets way too stuffy, so…"

"Right, right, take it off! It should be no problem for you."

"*Kksshh*. Yeah, that's right, they don't hang down or lose their shape at all! Okay, I won't hold back—"

"Why are you taking thaaaaaaaaaat off?!"

"Because you told me to?"

"I was talking about your gas mask! Not your bra!"

"*Kksshh*…what the…? That's what you meant?! You're so confusing…"

"You're the confusing one! Are you kinky?! Just like I suspected?! A kinky pervert?!"

"Now, now. I'll give you this, so don't get mad."

"No thank you!"

Ayaka brushed away the underwear and glared at Renko.

"…*Fwah*," Eiri yawned.

"Oh goodness me…" Maina smiled enviously. "They're really close friends, aren't they?"

Watching their friendly banter, Kyousuke had a feeling that they would be able to manage one way or another…

This most recent uproar had certainly broadened Ayaka's horizons. And it now looked like Ayaka herself was willing to broaden them even further. If so, she would surely be able to change.

Gradual change would be good.

It would be difficult for Kyousuke if he was on his own, but here he had friends like Eiri, Maina, and Renko to support him. Actually, Kyousuke hadn't been the one to stop his little sister. Renko had.

"...I completely misunderstood her..." Kyousuke groaned. He'd spent more time with his little sister than anyone else. She was more important to him than anything in the whole world...and he had failed to understand her. That fact sent a dull pang running through his heart.

Ayaka had said, "I depended on you too much." *That goes the same for me, doesn't it?* Until now, Kyousuke had been living only for his little sister. "...I guess I have to change, too."

"Hm? What's wrong, Kyousuke?" Renko asked. "You look so gloomy."

But Kyousuke only continued muttering to himself.

"Ah!" Renko seemed to reach some understanding on her own, and thrust out her right hand. "You wanted this, didn't you? Here you go!"

She held out the bra that she had removed earlier. Maybe because her cup size was too big, it wasn't in the academy-assigned striped pattern, but instead a very grown-up-looking black lace affair.

Pulling his eyes off the underwear, Kyousuke pushed Renko's hand away. "I don't want that, dummy...geez. You have a really crazy way of doing things, you know that, Renko?"

"Hm? Kyousuke, your face is turning red for some reason."

"Shut up! Hurry up and put it back on."

Kyousuke turned his back on Renko. His chest was pounding. It wasn't because he had seen her underwear. She had used her seductive techniques on him many times before, but the throbbing heartbeat that he was feeling now was something entirely different—

"Big brother..." A tug on Kyousuke's shirttail pulled him back to his senses.

Ayaka stood on tiptoe and brought her mouth close to his ear. "...I'm rooting for you," she whispered.

His heart skipped a beat. Even without asking, he knew just what Ayaka had meant—and he began to panic. "Rooting for me? You..."

"Yep! Your little sister is rooting for you, big brother. You are my family, after all, and I want you to be happy. And for that to happen, you need to get the best partner, right? As your little sister, I have a duty to help you do that. I have to keep an eye out and protect you from inferior women, let you know when you find a good one, and be your moral support..." Ayaka lowered her voice conspiratorially. "I promise not to stand in the way of your romance, big brother—I'm going to help you! Hee-hee-hee!"

Ayaka glanced over at the black gas mask. It was very clear who Ayaka thought would make the best partner (tentatively).

"O-oh..." A cold sweat broke out on Kyousuke's back. "If we fall in love with each other, she'll kill me, you know!"

"Don't worry. She promised to endure!"

"...I don't know."

She said a lot of other things after that. Even with Ayaka's support, Renko might not be able to persevere... So thinking, Kyousuke galvanized himself.

He needed to keep his mind far away from Renko and the fact that his heart quickened whenever he thought of her...

Secret Track

Inhuman screams roared through the red-tinged room.

A white arm waved like a flash, and the noise stopped.

"…It's me," answered a sweetly lisping Lolita voice.

Kurumiya sat at her office desk, illuminated by the setting sun. She had been preparing test questions before the interruption. Now she pressed her cell phone to her ear.

The wide-eyed cat on her phone strap swung back and forth like the corpse of a hanged man.

"……"

Silence. She waited a little while, but there was no response.

Kurumiya's brow wrinkled. She drummed the desk with her fingers. "Hey, I said it's me! Weren't you listening?"

"*Yes,*" a clear soprano voice finally answered. "*I heard you, Hijiri dear.*"

"Well if you heard me, then hurry up and answer, moron."

"*Sorry, sorry. It's because your voice is so cute. I was simply entranced.*"

"…Shut up. I'm not letting you waste my time."

"*Oh, are you shy?*"

"Let it go. Do you want to die?"

"*Even you can't kill me through the phone! Heh-heh…*"

"Wanna bet?" She clicked her tongue and leaned back in her chair.

"*…At any rate, it's been a long time, Hijiri dear. Are you well?*"

"Yeah, I'm having lots of fun. You?"

"*Uh-uh, I'm not doing too well. My target is particularly stubborn.*"

"Seems that way, huh? I heard they're no ordinary person. It's understandable if it's *that thing's mother.*"

"*…That thing?*"

"Yeah. The same one we talked about before. The boy who dumb idiot Renko fell for."

"_____"

The presence on the other end of the phone seemed to change. When the voice eventually answered, it was in a somewhat lower tone. "*…Ah, that one. Kyousuke Kamiya, was it? Is she still head over heels for him?*"

"Apparently. Actually, it's getting worse. She's madly in love."

The voice on the other end crackled. "*Hmmm…is that so? They can't possibly be dating… If he ever returns her feelings, her dormant murderous impulses will awaken, and she'll kill him, isn't that right?*"

"Should be. She keeps saying that herself."

"*But…but?! Have they gone as far as holding hands? Skinship and so on? They haven't…kissed yet, right? Of course they haven't, right?! If they have…oh, what'll we do!*"

"I dunno. Don't ask me. But—"

Kurumiya waited a moment for the person on the other end of the line to stop talking.

"Renko disobeyed my orders."

"*…Oh? What, did you try to have her kill Kyousuke again?*"

"No. This time it was his little sister. I ordered Renko to *nearly kill the girl in front of her brother.*"

Kurumiya had given Ayaka the shotgun, and while she was learning to handle it at the shooting range—Kurumiya had also given Renko her orders:

Turn the tables on Ayaka while Kyousuke was watching. This would make Renko truly want to kill and drive her to finally go through with the act, allowing them to assess the true value of Kyousuke's little sister should she survive…

If Ayaka, on the other hand, had been successful in killing Renko, it would have certainly shaken Kyousuke up. And even if Eiri or Maina had gotten killed in the process, in the end the only conversation would have been about how capable Ayaka must be.

Also, Kyousuke would probably never forgive Renko if she laid a hand on his little sister. Renko's love would end in a broken heart, and the whole abnormality would be resolved. No matter how it went, there would be a benefit.

That was how she'd meant for it to go, anyway.

"But she disobeyed my orders. I released the lock on her limiter beforehand so that it wouldn't matter whether it unlocked itself or not…but she stifled her own murderous impulses, and, far from tormenting the little sister, she *helped* her. I didn't hear her reasons for doing so, but maybe she was afraid…not of my punishment, but afraid that Kamiya might hate her. This is a serious situation! The Murder Maid—a total killing machine—resisted the urge to kill. That shouldn't be possible."

"……*That's right.*"

"Like I thought, putting her in school was a mistake. Letting a tool pretend to be human was…I also understand your feelings on the matter, but—"

"*Hijiri.*" The voice was gentle, yet authoritative. "*What you say is quite right. You are entirely correct. However, we've known it all from the beginning. You didn't think you could understand something that I didn't, did you?*"

"……Hm."

Pride was audible in her voice. There was not, however, any disrespect. Her intellect was far greater than Kurumiya—or anyone else—could possibly imagine. And though she often offended people, it almost never happened because of pride.

"…I'm sorry," said Kurumiya. "It seems that I misspoke."

"*Yes. There are things that I know that I don't want to know, you see? That girl is the organization's tool. She's certainly not a person. I know it's strange that the tool's creator would put her in school as though she were a human being. Even they think so! But I—*"

The voice on the other end choked up, and for a moment, an uncomfortable silence descended over them.

"Ah…it's just…," Kurumiya mumbled. "That is to say…I'm trying to take your side here! But you have to understand, after the first appearance of abnormalities big enough to interfere with normal operations, the higher-ups wouldn't keep quiet. Regardless of your intentions as her creator, as of now, Renko is—"

"*Hm? Sorry, I went to get a Monster Energy drink.*"

"Oh, piss off."

"*I said I was sorry! You know I have a chronic condition that makes me want to act out whenever things get too serious.*"

"Is that so? You'd better get to a hospital right away."

"*Ah-ha-ha! Impossible, I'm afraid. I'm busy.*"

"…Hmph. Playing a game of tag with your target? Well, don't work too hard."

"Mmm. Right now we're just playing hide-and-seek, though! It appears my target also has connections in the criminal underground… it's taking more work than I expected. Well, I'm really just here as a chaperone, but it honestly does feel like a vacation. I even got you a souvenir, Hijiri dear."

"Oh, thank you. Send it right along."

The stuffed animal hanging from Kurumiya's cell phone had also been a present from her friend. It was the mascot character for the melodic death metal band the Black Cat Murder, and she even had set her ringtone to play one of the band's songs. She was very pleased with it. Kurumiya's tastes often lined up with those of this particular friend, and she was looking forward to the delivery.

"No."

"…………"

The meaning of this easy rejection wasn't clear.

Perhaps sensing Kurumiya's disappointment, the person on the other line continued quickly. "Wait, wait! I'm not going to send it. I want to deliver it in person."

"…In person?"

"Yes. I've been thinking about it for a long time, and after hearing your stories, I don't want to put it off any longer. I'm coming to see you, Hijiri dear. I'll leave my target to someone else for a while, and come back to see Renko. That's what you want, isn't it?"

"……Mmm." It was as her friend had said. Renko's disorder was serious; it was out of Kurumiya's hands. She was grateful that the creator would come. "That's right. It'll help."

"Yes. Since I'll be in charge, you can relax and drink your milk. It would be good to see some growth by the time I got back."

"…Bitch. As soon you get here, I'm taking you down."

"Ehh?! But I was talking about Renko…heh-heh! It's been almost half a year… I'm really looking forward to it! To seeing you and Renko, of course, but also that—Kyousuke Kamiya you mentioned. I also definitely want to meet the object of my daughter's first love. I have so many questions! Like 'Why did you fall for her?' and 'How hard did you fall?' and 'What do you think of Renko?' and so on…though I doubt I'll approve of any of his answers." The voice was laughing but did not seem especially relaxed.

Kurumiya smiled unconsciously. *She called the tool her "daughter."* Her attachment to Renko reminded Kurumiya of a doting parent.

"Well, that's about all, so…I'm looking forward to seeing you! I'll call again soon."

"Sure. You're real delicate, so take care of yourself."

"And you're awfully tough, Hijiri dear, so you take care as well. Bye-bye now!"

"Yeah, later."

—Click.

The line cut off.

With a sigh, Kurumiya lowered the phone from her ear. Then, quite suddenly, she started laughing. The sun had already set, leaving the room in shadow. The only point of light was the cell phone, lying discarded on the desk.

The bright screen displayed her call history, at the top of which was a name:

Reiko Hikawa…

Psycome 3: Murder Maiden and the
Fatal Final / End

AFTERWORD   Master of Ceremonies

Hello, or should I say, "How do you do?" I am Mizuki Mizushiro.

Continuing with the theme of "Cutthroats" and "Killer Queens," this third volume features a "Fatal Family Member." Kyousuke's little sister, Ayaka, who ran in the background of Volumes 1 and 2, now becomes the main story. This is liable to lead to some troubling developments, but that's romantic comedy for you. I exercised my ingenuity so that you could laugh and enjoy, without feeling like it gets too brutal. I tried to keep the balance between "psycho" and "comedy" in mind.

Anyway, currently the *Psycome* promotional video is being made public! They also made background music for it—it's just ordinary death metal vocals. The hook is a little out there. Is this really a love comedy...? If you like, please enjoy the music and stylish visuals that will leave you guessing.

Well, then. Each time the afterword is one page, so here are all the thank-yous.

To the person in charge, Ms. Gibu; the illustrator, Namanie; the designers at musicago graphics; the proofreaders; the PR team; my friends; my family; all of my relatives; everyone who had anything to do with the publication of this book; all of the readers who kindly read and support *Psycome*; and you, who have now picked up this book. Truly, thank you!

The next volume, which is scheduled to arrive in the winter features "the Assassins"—Eiri's family will become the main story.

Mizuki Mizushiro
~Written while listening to Architects~

Little Chihiro is looking
forward to Volume 4.
Sluuurrrp...

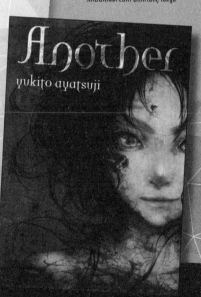